RUNHIDESEEK

THE FIRST BOOK IN THE TRILOGY

D1113867

GABBY TYE

Text Copyright © 2013 Gabby Tye
Cover image © 2013 Eliza Teoh
Back cover image © 2013 Nicholas Chew Ken Min
Book design by Serene See

First published in August 2013 by
Bubbly Books Pte Ltd
40c Hongkong Street
Singapore 059679

Website: www.bubbly-books.com
Email: info@bubbly-books.com

A CIP record of this book is available from the
National Library Board (Singapore)

ISBN 978-981-07-7222-2

FOR MOO

The funny thing about losing your memory, if losing your memory can be considered funny at all, is that useless memories stick in your brain while the important stuff disappears. Important stuff like what your name is. Or where you live. Or what happened to make you lose your memory.

CHAPTER 1

Oh, I know that I am in Singapore, that I grew up in Singapore and have lived here all my life. I know that I am 15 years old, but can't remember my birthday. I remember other stupid things like: I had parents and friends and that I was a student.

I remember what school was – sitting in class, boring lessons, and even more boring teachers. And TV shows I liked to watch. But I can't remember who my parents were. Did I have brothers? Sisters? Who was my best friend? What school did I go to? Who were my teachers? I have no clue. For goodness sakes, why can't I have forgotten about school?

The worst thing was, a little after I regained consciousness, I got a very strong feeling that there was something I was supposed to do. Something important, something big. But as hard as I tried, I could not remember what it was. I also found myself in a very strange situation, one that I knew could not be normal, even though I couldn't quite remember what normal was...

But let me start from the beginning. This whole thing started two days ago.

Yes, I still remember how to count. And read a calendar. And tell the time.

It was December 2, 2037. It was a Wednesday morning...

I opened my eyes and found myself lying in a puddle of muddy water. I tried to stand up but fell back to the ground, gasping in pain. My eyes registered the devastation around me. Nothing was familiar. I couldn't recognise anything.

CHAPTER 2

"Mommy? Daddy...? Where am I...? What's going on...?"

Yes, so you know. The first thing I did was call for my mother. A 15-year-old girl calling for her mama. Big deal. If you had seen what I did, you would have called for your mother too. Then I fainted.

The next time I opened my eyes, I'm guessing a few hours had passed. I was lying on an uncomfortable sofa. It smelled funny. Like a wet, smelly dog. It seemed that my memory loss didn't affect my sense of smell. Too bad for me.

"Hey, guys, she's awake!"

I found myself staring into a pair of green eyes belonging to a boy about my age or slightly older. He had longish brown hair and a nice face. Cute, I thought. He had a slight build but looked pretty strong. I noticed a bandage on his left arm stretching from his elbow all the way up to his shoulder.

"Are you okay, sweet pea?" he asked, his brows furrowing. I could see the concern in his unusually dark green eyes.

Sweet pea?

"Yeah," I nodded uneasily. "I'm fine."

"I'm Jae, who're you?" The look of concern changed into a questioning one.

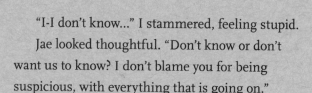

"I-I don't know..." I stammered, feeling stupid.

Jae looked thoughtful. "Don't know or don't want us to know? I don't blame you for being suspicious, with everything that is going on."

I heard a whisper. "She looks suspicious. I don't trust her."

"How did she get here? Why haven't we seen her around?" I heard someone else murmur.

Jae's face hardened suddenly and his look turned into a glare. "Whatever. We'll let you have some time to decide if you want to let us know who you are. Just know that you are safe with us."

Safe from what? Again, there was that nagging feeling. I looked over his shoulder and saw heads nodding vigorously. There were about 15 boys and girls, all around my age or slightly younger, as far as I could tell. They looked like an odd bunch. Most of them looked a little worse for wear. Their clothes were dirty and they looked unwashed and untidy.

I glanced around. We seemed to be in the backyard of someone's house.

The sofa I was lying on was under a shelter that jutted out from the back of the house. Beyond the shelter, there was a big garden. Quite impressive to have such a big garden in Singapore, I thought. But apart from mud and a line of

pathetic dried-up palm trees, it was totally bare –
no grass, no shrubs, no flowers, no chirping birds,
nothing. It was utterly empty.

I heard someone whisper, "Quite pretty."

I blushed. Jae must have seen me redden. He
stiffened and glared at the boy. "Seriously?" he said.

Okaaay, then. I guess he thought I wasn't pretty.
Whatever. I changed my mind. He didn't look so
cute after all.

Jae frowned and looked at me from head to toe, a
look of distaste on his face.

"Kyl," he said, addressing a boy standing apart
from the rest, "get her some clean clothes."

I looked down at myself and blushed again,
wrapping my arms around my chest. My T-shirt
was filthy. And wet. Showing off everything! Argh.
My jeans were so caked in mud I couldn't bend
my knees. I also saw that I was barefoot. My eyes
travelled to the crowd of kids all gawking at me.
I noticed that they were all barefoot too.

I looked at Jae's feet. No shoes.

Had I just woken up in some weird alternate
universe where no one wore shoes? Even though I had
about a million and two questions whirling in my head,
the foremost being – Dude, where are your shoes? –
I decided to keep my mouth shut for the moment.

I was led into the back of the house and into a tiny stinking toilet to change. For the second time that day, I lamented that I hadn't lost my sense of smell. The stench was incredibly bad.

CHAPTER 3

Kyl had gotten me a T-shirt that was two sizes too big and a pair of jeans that fit okay – and by okay I really mean that they didn't make my butt look big. Strange, isn't it, how people obsess about trivial things, even in dire situations?

I looked around the filthy toilet. I really needed to pee, but the toilet was beyond gross. Streaks of grime ran down the inside – and outside – of the toilet bowl. I wrinkled my nose. I tried the flush. It didn't work. Which explained the pail of water and the plastic scoop next to the toilet.

I sighed. If you gotta go, you gotta go. I peed, and then flushed it down with some water. I turned on the tap. No water. Sighing again, I scooped some water from the pail and washed my hands over the sink. What on earth was going on?

I took stock of the situation: I didn't know who I was. I didn't know where I was. I was stuck in a house with a bunch of weird kids who didn't wear shoes. Maybe I was on that show that played stupid gags on unsuspecting victims. Maybe someone would jump out with a camera and say, "Ha, we got you!" But that wouldn't explain how I couldn't remember anything. Think! Think! Think! I told myself.

I looked into the streaky mirror and saw an unfamiliar face staring back at me. The face in the mirror was pretty. Whoever made that comment earlier was right. I didn't think I was being immodest. Considering that I was practically seeing my own face for the first time, I think I was being quite objective.

The face in the mirror had fair skin, a nice straight small nose, nice high cheekbones and long black hair that hung all the way down my back. Although, at the moment, it was tangled and streaked with mud.

But it was my eyes that caught my attention. They were big, clear and beautiful – and a deep shade of violet. Interesting, I thought, because it gave me a glimpse into who I was.

Now this I remembered – that in Singapore, parents could choose the colour of their child's hair and eyes (among other traits), even before their baby was born. But not everyone could afford such genetic manipulations, of course. Only the rich folks.

Which means, I must have come from a rather rich home.

As I thought about this, a memory suddenly flashed into my mind. I saw the devastation I had woken up to earlier that day. I saw the awful scene with an uncanny clarity. Where was memory loss when you needed it? I had woken up in the middle of a muddy patch on the side of a road in the middle of a Housing Board estate. It could have been Toa Payoh, or Yishun or Woodlands. All government flats kind of looked the same, didn't they?

Here was the awful part: the estate was in complete ruin. Some blocks of flats were burnt from top to bottom. Others were simply abandoned. There was no one about. And I mean no one, even though it was clearly day time. No pedestrians, no cars, no dogs barking. Just silence. The row of shophouses in front of me was thrashed – shutters were left open, glass doors and plate-glass windows were smashed. There was rubbish everywhere.

I felt my knees go weak at the memory. What had happened out there? I decided I had no choice. I had to trust Jae and Kyl and those kids, whoever they were. I took a deep breath – which I realised immediately was a stupid thing to do in a reeking toilet – and opened the door.

The first person I found was Jae, because he was right outside the toilet. He was leaning on the wall trying to look aloof, but not quite succeeding. I felt slightly annoyed.

"What took you so long?" he asked.

CHAPTER 4

He looked at my oversized T-shirt and shrugged. "Beggars can't be choosers. We don't have a lot of clothes to spare."

And shoes? What about shoes, I thought. And before I could help myself, words came pouring out of my mouth in a confused rush. "I wasn't kidding earlier. I really can't remember anything. I don't know who I am. I don't know where I am. I don't know what happened. I don't understand what is happening. Are we at war? Is Singapore at war? Why haven't I seen a grown-up around here? Tell me!"

"You really don't know, do you? You really remember nothing?"

"Are you trying to annoy me? I just said I remember nothing! Do you have any idea how hard it is to wake up and remember nothing?" I was shouting, even though I hadn't meant to. I guess losing your memory can be stressful. Then to my horror, I felt tears prickling at the corner of my eyes. Good grief, I started to cry.

Jae, like the boy he was, looked alarmed and didn't know what to do. He patted my arm awkwardly.

"I'm really sorry this happened to you, okay? Try to calm down and I'll explain everything as best as I can. Don't cry," he said, looking confused.

He looked so helpless I laughed. Then I cried some more. Then I laughed. I must have looked really crazy.

"How about we decide on a name for you first?" he asked, trying to snap me out of my crying-laughing fit. "How about Ashley?"

Through my tears, I glared at him.

"No? Erm... Brenda?"

I glared at him some more. How many lame names could one boy come up with?

"Still no? I know! Cassandra! Okay?" Jae looked at me hopefully. "Doreen?"

I continued to glare at him. I really wasn't in the mood to play name games. "Are you going to go down the entire alphabet? Why don't we just skip to Z so I can reject all your stupid ideas?"

"Whoa! There's no need to be mean. I'm only trying to help." It was his turn to snap at me. "Fine! I'm going to call you Zee."

"Wha...? No!" I said, but it was too late.

"She should be thankful I didn't call her an S," he muttered as he walked away.

"I heard that," I growled at him, although I wasn't really angry with him, just very confused. Zee didn't sound too bad. He was just trying to be nice, I thought. Get a hold of yourself! Stop acting like a nut.

"Yeah, whatever. Call me Zee," I managed to say, running to catch up with him as he walked into the house.

With some effort, I pulled myself together and forced a smile.

"What's for lunch?" I asked when I caught up with him.

Jae turned to me and raised an eyebrow. "You don't know who you are or where you came from and the only thing you can think about is food!?"

CHAPTER 5

I glanced at him and said, "Yeah."

He laughed out loud, his green eyes twinkling with amusement. I couldn't help but notice how cute he was. I also noticed through his tatty T-shirt that he had a nice lean body and long muscular arms. He looked like he could have been an Olympic swimmer.

"Hey, is it really that funny? I feel like I haven't eaten properly in months."

"Maybe it's because you haven't," he said seriously. He stopped laughing.

I didn't know whether to believe him or not.

Suddenly, colours flashed in front of me and I fell to my knees, clutching my head in my hands.

"Zee! Are you okay?" I heard Jae say. I felt him grab me as I fell.

In my mind, I saw people running. I smelled smoke. Someone was crying out my name in panic. Shoving, pushing, panic. Then, nothing.

I opened my eyes and found myself lying on the floor, in Jae's arms. He was looking at me all concerned. "Are you okay? Do you know what happened? Your eyes glazed over and then you passed out."

I grabbed his arm. "My name! I just heard it! What is it?"

He frowned. "How am I supposed to know? Are you okay?"

"I-I'm fine. Just a little dizzy." His arms around me felt quite nice, I had to admit. More importantly, I had heard my name, I was sure of it. But every time I tried to grasp it, it slipped out of reach.

Jae looked unconvinced. He raised an eyebrow, but said, "Okay then... we'd better get you some food."

He helped me up and made sure I was steady on my feet before letting me go. His startling green eyes studied me carefully. I felt a faint feeling of recognition and a sudden affinity to him. He reminded me of something. I just couldn't remember what.

Since we were at the back of the house, he led me through the kitchen into the dining area, which opened out into the living room. Even though the house was clearly run down, I could tell that it had once been beautiful. Some rich dude must have lived here.

CHAPTER 6

A crystal chandelier hung over the long wooden dining table, although it was covered in dust. The living room floor was expensive marble that felt cool under my bare feet and the walls were covered in a flowery wallpaper. A plush sofa set was positioned in front of a humongous flat-screen multi-viewer TV, one that covered the entire wall. But it wasn't turned on.

"A wall-to-wall MV. Cool," I commented. Now we were talking. At least this dump had entertainment, I thought.

"We don't have electricity," Jae said, following my gaze. "No one has."

Great. So, no MV. Sigh.

My eyes were drawn back to the dining table where some of the kids were laying out the food. I was so hungry. Everything came out of tins, and everything seemed like it should be eaten from tins. There was a huge tin of sardines in the middle of the table. There were also tinned sausages, tinned chicken curry, tinned tuna and tinned lychees. Jae handed me a fork and an empty sardine tin to use as a bowl.

"We don't use plates because we don't want to waste water washing them. This way, we simply throw away the tins. Keep that fork and don't lose it. You'll need it for every meal. Plus I'm not sharing mine with you," he said.

He was suddenly very curt and cold. I rolled my eyes. Whatever. Boys could be so strange.

Something told me I hated tinned food, but I was so hungry I didn't care. I tried every "dish" and went back for seconds. All the other kids joined in. Despite the weirdness of the situation, we were soon joking and kidding around. We were kids, after all.

There weren't enough seats, so we all sat on the floor. Everyone introduced themselves, but – surprise, surprise – I couldn't remember them all. It was not a case of memory loss this time. There were simply too many faces and names to remember.

But some kids stood out, mostly because they were closer to my own age. There were 15 of us in all, me included. The youngest child there was 10. The oldest were Kyl and Jae, who were 16.

There was Eryn, who was 13. I liked her straightaway because she reminded me of an inquisitive mouse. She was small for her age and very quiet, but had bright intelligent eyes and a ready smile.

There was Brion, who was 15, like me. He seemed to be the joker in the group, constantly

cracking jokes to get the other kids laughing. Actually, he looked really geeky with his pale skin and neat slicked-back hair. Had short-sightedness not been genetically eradicated, I bet he would have been wearing super thick glasses.

There was a tough-looking girl called Dyanne, also 15. I caught her staring at me, a strange look in her eyes. Her best friend Shulin sat next to her. Or maybe they were sisters because they looked so similar. They both had blue eyes and orangey-red hair chopped really short. They were both tall and thin.

I couldn't tell what race any of these kids were. But that was not so surprising. With all the genetic experimenting that had been going on, and the ridiculous choices parents had been making, it was no longer possible to tell a person's race by looking at them.

I wonder what Dyanne and Shulin's parents had been thinking when they picked blue eyes and red hair. At least my parents had good taste, I mused. Black hair and violet eyes was an awesome combination.

Then it struck me that Kyl looked the most Asian. He was the only one with black hair and black eyes. Either his parents were one of those purists who refused to modify – or "mod" – their babies, or they were simply too poor to pay for the genetic procedures.

"Okay," I finally said, through a mouthful of tuna. "I'm ready to talk. What's going on? Who's in charge of this place? And what happened to all the grown-ups?"

That was a conversation stopper. Everyone grew silent and looked uncomfortably at one another.

"What?" I said, stupidly ignorant.

Kyl sounded grim. "No one's in charge. Don't you remember anything? We've all been abandoned. So far, this is the safest place we have found in the last few weeks."

"Abandoned?" I said. "What do you mean? Why did your parents abandon you? My parents would never do that to me!"

Kyl looked awkward. "I hate to tell you this way, and I'm really sorry, but it is true. All the adults are gone. We have been left to die."

"What?" My mind reeled. Here we were, a bunch of kids sitting in an abandoned house, eating dinner from tins. And if that wasn't bad enough, this boy, this stranger, had to dump this nasty bombshell on me – we had been left to die?

CHAPTER 7

"What are you talking about? Why?" I demanded.

Kyl took a deep breath. "Okay. Let's go right back to the start. Do you remember when we were kids – I mean when we were really little – the Green Movement was really strong? All that stuff about recycling everything, and wasting nothing?"

I nodded, so he continued.

"About two years ago, a new movement called TNI or The Nature Initiative became really popular. They were concerned about the way food was produced around the world. People were campaigning against genetically-modified vegetables and fruits. They were protesting against the way animals were injected with antibiotics in commercial farms. They warned that one day, all this human meddling with nature would bring unintended consequences. Do you remember any of this?"

I nodded again. It all sounded kind of familiar.

"Do you recall protests that were held at feedlots around the world, where they showed us places where animals were crammed together and bred in filthy conditions and stuffed with food?" Kyl carried on. "They said we were being sold meat from animals that were sick or dying. And that sooner or later, humans would be affected in terrible ways?"

I had only vague memories.

"And do you remember cloning?" Kyl said. "Many farmers had begun to breed cows, lamb, poultry and other animals through cloning. But the problem with the new animal variants was, they could not reproduce. Try as they might, scientists and farmers could not make cloned females reproduce. So they tried inter-breeding cloned animals with normal animals.

"But that made things worse because now, the normal healthy animals could not reproduce either! So that's what you get for messing with nature, said the TNI. They warned of terrible consequences again, that all animals and maybe humans too were going to become sterile."

"Don't forget the thing about genetically-modified vegetables and fruit," Jae said, continuing for Kyl. Scientists had by now perfected such oddities as giant potatoes, carrots and other root vegetables weighing as much as 10kg each. There were also rot-resistant berries, leafy vegetables that stayed crisp for months and even new varieties of fruit created in a lab like the skinless orange and the blue apple.

"Do you remember the Duya?" It was a cross between the durian and the papaya; a durian without the prickly shell. Singaporeans loved it, he said. But small pockets of people started developing allergies to these new types of food, and of course, TNI warned of yet another doomsday scenario – we would die from eating these "fake" foods.

To Kyl, I said, "To be honest, I never really paid much attention to what they said."

"Neither did most of us," Jae agreed, "until their warnings started to come true."

31

Suddenly, Dyanne spoke up, "Don't you understand? It all really did come true. Look around you. Everything's dead. Everything!"

The kids around her patted her sympathetically. They all looked glum now. Some kids were crying silently.

CHAPTER 8

"Tell me how it happened," I urged Jae to continue.

"It started with the animals in the farms, labs and feedlots. They started dying off really quickly. No one had time to react. The same thing happened in every country. Almost overnight, there was no meat left. The organic farmers, those that stuck to farming naturally, were the only ones with live animals. There was a rush to save those animals, but it was too late. Those animals died too."

"When was this?" I interrupted.

"About five months ago," Kyl said softly, his voice tinged with sadness.

"I have no memory of all this," I said pathetically.

"Lucky you," Shulin said, rather meanly, I thought. But she had tears in her eyes, so I bit back the retort that threatened to escape my lips.

"Then what happened?" I asked.

Jae continued the horrible story. "It started happening to the plants and vegetation too. Everything was dying. TNI had been proven right. Governments all over the world were scrambling to find answers. Some were denying anything was amiss. Until the babies started dying. Old people too. Do you notice that there are no young kids here?"

I looked around, horrified. Death sounded like such a foreign idea to me. It felt so unreal. How could this have happened? I wanted Jae to stop right then. I didn't want to know anymore. But he went on anyway.

"We don't know what it was. Was it a virus that killed them? Or was it from all the bad food? No one told us. To cut a long story short, many people have died. Those that are left have no more food to eat. There is no more food left on earth. No more live food, at least, which explains this," he said, holding up an empty sardine tin.

"This is what you mean when you said the adults have abandoned us? They've all died?" I said, a lump rising in my throat. Even though I couldn't remember my parents, I felt a sense of loss.

This time, it was Kyl who cut in. "No, they are alive. Well, not many, but the ones that survived decided to save themselves and not us," he said grimly.

"My mom would never abandon me!" I said. I believed it too. I felt it in my heart. Even though I couldn't remember her face, I remembered being loved and treasured by my mother.

To my outburst, Jae only grunted cynically. "Some adults didn't agree, but they didn't have a choice. If they disagreed, they would simply have been left on the outside, like us."

"Outside what?" I asked, not really wanting to know. I just wanted the whole thing to go away, like a bad dream.

"Outside Camp Zero," Jae said.

I woke up the next day and found myself on the floor, packed in tight with a whole roomful of sleeping girls. For one minute, I was completely disorientated and confused. Where was I?

Then I remembered.

CHAPTER 9

Unfortunately, I only remembered what had happened the day before. I still had no memory of what got me here. I sighed. I felt exhausted. I felt as if there was a big weight sitting on my shoulders, one I could not shake off.

I looked around the room again. Apart from me, there were seven girls, all lined up side by side. The room was quite big and there were two small beds pushed against the wall. Dyanne was sleeping on one of the beds and another girl, I think it was Shulin, was sleeping on the other. The rest of us were sleeping on mattresses, blankets, cushions and pillows.

I thought about what had happened the day before. Jae and the other kids had started telling me about Camp Zero, and what they thought went on in there. But it was so unreal and horrible that I couldn't take it anymore and ran upstairs to explore the house instead.

Although I had been too distracted to really pay attention, I did take in the fact that there were four bedrooms upstairs – two on each side of an open landing that looked like it had once been a children's toy area. Colourful children's cabinets lined one wall and broken, dirty toys were strewn everywhere.

The toilets were all marble – marble bathtubs, marble basins and marble floors. You could tell that the previous owners had abandoned their home in a hurry. There were still shampoo bottles and toothbrushes lying around. The kids had explained that there were homes like this all over Singapore, homes that were still usable. Over the last two months or so, they had been wandering all over, moving from house to house, surviving on whatever food that had been left behind.

This current house was a terrace house, flanked on both sides by other houses. They had chosen it completely by chance. Kyl had liked the fact that it was surrounded by a high wall. To their amazement, the house had produced a rare treasure – an entire pantry filled with food.

The owners must have planned to weather the disaster at home, judging from all the food they had stored. There were cartons of instant noodles, sacks of rice, shelves and shelves of canned food and huge bottles of water. There was also a hydro-powered radio receiver, several torches and spare batteries as well as a huge cache of candles.

"Why didn't you just stay in one place?" I had asked.

"If you haven't noticed, the toilets aren't working," Dyanne said, rolling her eyes.

"Oh," I replied lamely.

The kids moved to a new house every time the toilets started getting seriously backed up, or the mess became too much, whichever came first. They were kids, and kids with no grown-ups around meant that no one did any cleaning. Garbage was simply thrown out of windows or shoved into corners. The only things each kid had with them at all times were a pillow, a blanket, a set of cutlery and one set of clothes. They seemed pretty organised, I thought.

The shoes – it was finally explained to me – were always kept safe and dry on a high shelf because shoes were hard to find. While clothes could be found in any house, shoes in the right size were much harder to come by. So they had to be preserved as much as possible and the kids went about barefoot whenever they could.

It was still dark, and I had no idea what time it was. Everyone was still sleeping soundly, so I decided I might as well go back to sleep. I lay my head down on a musty but comfortable pillow and closed my eyes. But sleep didn't come.

Instead, I found myself thinking about Camp Zero. Even though I didn't believe what the kids said at first, it was starting to make sense, in an awful sort of way.

41

Camp Zero, they had explained, was located at Changi. The leaders of the country had planned to brave the looming disaster by building hundreds of emergency shelters at Camp Zero.

CHAPTER 10.

Tons of supplies were trucked into the area – bedding, medicine, medical equipment, food, water, diesel-powered electric generators, solar-powered generators. The idea was to move everyone into that area when things got really bad.

The police and military were the first to be moved into Camp Zero, because things were expected to be chaotic and someone needed to maintain order. But as the speed of the disaster took the whole world by surprise, it became clear that they simply didn't have time to build enough shelters.

Food was also a major worry. Even though the government had stockpiled huge amounts of rice and other basic food supplies, they estimated that they had only enough to feed two million people for six months. Or one million people for a year. Or half a million people for two years... You get the idea.

For a while, people assumed that the government would simply build shelters faster and buy more food. What they didn't realise was that worldwide, there wasn't any more food to be bought – at any price. When selected families started getting letters to move into Camp Zero, people started getting suspicious. Rumours started going around that only a few "chosen" families and individuals would be invited to live at Camp Zero, while the rest would be left to fend for themselves on the outside.

Fear set in. People started looting supermarkets and malls, grabbing everything and anything they could find – water, clothes, food. It was a real mess that ended in riots. Thousands of people were killed. But they were the lucky ones, because they didn't live to suffer the hunger and desperation that was to follow. Hordes of people started showing up at the doors of Camp Zero, demanding to be let in, only to be turned away by armed soldiers.

Within the first month, those on the outside slowly died off. Some of the stronger ones formed fierce roving gangs, gangs that would kill other gangs for food. Some were killed simply for the clothes or shoes they were wearing. The world was no longer a civilised place. It was a matter of survival.

Military trucks still patrolled the roads every day, but if they came across any skirmishes, they didn't intervene. The only thing the soldiers did was to pick up the bodies. This was still

Singapore, after all, Jae had said with a cynical laugh. The leaders couldn't bear to leave the bodies to rot where they were.

I felt sad thinking about it. And weary. I started to drift back to sleep when something jarred me awake.

From outside, I heard voices. They sounded angry. Curious, I crept out silently. The voices were coming from downstairs. I heard three separate voices. I slid myself into a crouch and looked down into the living room from the top of the stairs, careful not to be seen.

It was Kyl, Jae and Brion. They were sitting on the floor facing each other. Kyl was shouting.

"I hate you so much I hope you fall onto a fork."

"Well, I hate you so much I hope you fall into a fan and I get to turn it on!" Jae shouted back.

CHAPTER 11

"I hope a fridge falls on your head while you sleep," Brion yelled.

What? I shook my head, just in case I was dreaming. I was not.

"I hope you choke on a candy cane and it gets stuck in your throat," Kyl retorted. "Horizontally."

"I hope someone drops a pot of boiling hot pee on your head!" Jae said.

"I hope that when the both of you parachute out of a plane, you land in a bowl of needles," Brion snapped back.

They glared at each other, fuming. Their faces were tight with anger.

Brion broke the silence. "Why would anyone boil a pot of pee?"

"So that it can be poured over you, lamebrain," Jae said. "What about a bowl of needles? That makes even less sense. Where would you find a bowl that big?"

"I hope your ass gets bitten off by a wolf," Brion said, apparently moving the bizarre argument along.

"Your ass is so gross, no wolf would want to bite it," was Jae's reply.

"You two are so ugly, when you walk down the street, babies faint," Kyl interjected.

"You are so ugly, when your mother gave birth to you, the doctor vomited," Brion said.

"You're so ugly, when you go to watch a comedy, people cry," Jae shouted.

Kyl's mouth twitched. His shoulders shook. He burst out laughing. What on earth?

I felt a tug at my elbow. I jumped in fright, then relaxed when I saw that it was only Eryn.

"Who's winning?" she asked.

"Winning?"

"Yup. The game. Face-Off. They made it up. They do this all the time. They sit and hurl insults at each other to relieve stress," Eryn explained.

"How does insulting each other relieve stress?" I asked.

"They are the oldest here, and they feel responsible for all of us. It's a big burden and they used to get into fights with each other over what to do. That's how Jae got that big wound on his arm. It was Kyl. It was then that they decided that fighting was not very useful. We don't have medicine, so we can't afford to hurt each other. So they started Face-Off," she said.

It made sense, sort of. I asked Eryn, "So how does a person win this game?"

"The one who laughs first loses. The one who can keep a straight face the longest, wins."

I peered through the railing. Kyl was totally losing it. He was laughing quite hysterically. Brion and Jae sat stone-faced, staring at each other.

"You are so stupid, the dust ball on the floor is smarter than you," Brion said.

"You are so stupid, your brain grew an arm so it could slap itself," Jae replied.

Eryn giggled softly. "Another thing," she said, "no cussing allowed. That's a rule. Because of the little kids."

"Okaaay," I said.

"They are getting better at this. I've caught almost all their shows," she said, as if she was watching television. I guess there wasn't much to do in terms of entertainment, so this would have to do.

"I hope your brain shrivels up like a raisin and gets eaten by a donkey," Brion said.

"I hope your wee-wee shrivels up and falls off," Jae said.

"Wee-wee?" Eryn repeated. She clamped her hand over her mouth to stop herself from laughing out loud.

"Shh!" I warned, but I too was stifling my laughter.

By now, Kyl was rolling on the floor clutching his stomach. He laughed so hard he snorted.

"I bet you don't even have one," Brion continued.

"I bet you don't have an asshole. Because you're so full of shit," Jae shot back.

"Hey! No cussing!" Brion said.

"Asshole is not cussing. It is a noun. So is shit," Jae said, crossing his arms.

Eryn and I clutched each other, laughing silently.

Brion made a weird snort. He started to smile, but stopped himself. Jae's lips twitched. He was trying hard not to smile too. Kyl's laughter was too contagious. They both looked at him, then at each other. Soon, they exploded into laughter.

"C'mon. Let's get some rest," Kyl said after they managed to calm down. They stood up and made their way towards the stairs.

"Eee!" Eryn squeaked. She grabbed my hand and dragged me away before we got spotted. We stumbled into our room and shut the door, collapsing on the floor and giggling quietly.

"Shut up!" It was Dyanne. "Or I will come over and smash your heads!"

Yikes! We scrambled to our mattresses and lay down. I smiled to myself. I couldn't be sure, but I had the feeling that I hadn't laughed like that for a long time.

I clutched at my side painfully as I ran next to Jae.

"I knew you shouldn't have come," he said, glancing at me.

We were on a "hunting" expedition for more food. Breakfast had been really horrible, just half a can of baked beans each.

CHAPTER 12

And lunch had been worse – more sardines and jars of pickled vegetables that were salty and disgusting. I ate everything, nonetheless. It was then that I realised that the "feast" the night before had been a special one, just for me.

They normally ate as little as possible to preserve whatever food they had left. The stash in the house was dwindling, so when the kids started talking about venturing out to search for more food – something they took turns to do regularly – I volunteered to go. It was my way of thanking them. Plus, I didn't want them to start thinking of me as a burden, an extra mouth to feed. Dyanne had already voiced her objections to keeping me in their group.

"Why is she here, anyway? We can hardly feed ourselves! We're running out of food. We don't know who she is, so why must we help her?"

She had glanced around smugly to see if anyone else agreed with her. I looked around and saw a few kids nodding silently.

"You see? You all agree with..."

Kyl cut her off with a glare. "How could you? So now you think survival is more important than helping someone? More important than living an honourable life? Who knows what

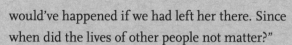

would've happened if we had left her there. Since when did the lives of other people not matter?"

Dyanne backed down, but looked defiant.

Another kid spoke up, "If we don't have enough to eat, we will all die. I don't want to die."

"But if we leave her to die, won't we be like the ones in Camp Zero? Saving themselves and leaving others to die?" Jae said. "We all have a choice, you know. And our choices define who we are. I don't want to be one of them."

"Why are you defending her, anyway?" Dyanne said. "Just because she's pretty? You talk about honour, but it is so clear that you stupid boys are all suckers for a pretty face!"

"That's not true," Eryn said quietly. "I want her to stay too. It wouldn't be right to let another kid die. Haven't we seen enough kids die? What if it were Shulin? What if we lost her one day, and another group found her and left her to die instead of helping her? How would you feel then?"

That seemed to have an effect on Dyanne. Her face took on a stubborn look, but I saw a deep sadness in her eyes.

"We have to give her a chance at least," Kyl said. "She could be useful. Another set of hands also means more work can be done."

So Jae and I had just stolen some food –
although in my mind, it wasn't really stealing
if people had abandoned their stuff. We had
rummaged through the homes in an HDB
block and were about to run away with our loot
when three adults ambushed us and tried to take
our food.

They jumped us when we rounded a corner
at the void deck and tried to grab at our bags
of food. We should have known better, and we
should have been more alert, but we were tired
from searching house to house, climbing all
those stairs.

We ran from them as fast as we could,
turning a corner where Jae pulled me into a small
enclosed space, where we stayed hidden. There
we sat, gasping for air until the sound of angry
footsteps faded.

I turned and glared at Jae, trying to
ignore the fact that we were standing so close.
"That wouldn't have happened if you had listened
to what I said, but no, you had to do it your way
and now look what happened."

Jae had insisted on being super thorough.
He had made us start from the very top floor –
the 25th floor, in this case – and we had to go

through every single flat. Being the impatient one, I had wanted to leave after finding a nice stash of canned food and instant noodles on the 20th floor. But no, Jae said, we had to look in every flat.

Jae shot me a sheepish half-grin. "Look, tulip, I'm sorry, okay? But it's not my fault, you agreed to do it too."

Tulip? I scowled at him. "Jerk."

"We should go back now, since we have everything we need. Also, they might have friends, so we'd better go before they bring back-up."

"Why don't they just look for their own food anyway, instead of stealing from us?" I asked.

"Firstly, they are too lazy and too weak to search the way we do. Secondly," he said, pausing to give me a smug look, "they can't pick locks like I can."

"Yeah, yeah, big applause for the master criminal," I said sarcastically. I refused to let him see how impressed I was with his lock-picking skills, which were really quite good. He had managed to open all kinds of locked doors and metal gates.

He looked faintly disappointed. "Enough chatting. We'd better go now."

"Fine, but give me something to fight with first, just in case. I bet you fight like a girl," I taunted needlessly. Why was I being so mean to Jae? Was I a mean person?

Jae peered around the space we were in. It was a small storage area filled with cleaning equipment – brooms and pails and stuff like that. He took hold of a mop and pulled off the head.

"Here, will this do?" he said, handing me the mop stick.

I sighed, taking the stick. "Do I have a choice? Let's go!"

Jae opened the door to the storage room slowly and looked out. He shut it really quickly and blew out a big breath.

"Not good," he said. "They brought back-up. There are 10 of them now."

CHAPTER 13

"So what do we do? Maybe we should just stay in here," I whispered.

"Chicken," he said, smirking at me. "Who's being the girl now?"

"I *am* a girl," I said, shooting daggers at him.

Before he could think of a comeback, the door to the storage room flew open and we found ourselves staring at a big man. He had a shaved head and tattoos running up his bulging arm muscles. He would have looked a lot scarier had he not been wearing a pink T-shirt.

As I stood and gawked, Jae grabbed a broom and shoved the dusty end into his face. As the man spluttered, Jae pushed him aside and ran out, grabbing me along.

We tried to run away but they had us surrounded. I gaped in horror at the men.

Jae and I stood back to back, each with a huge rucksack filled with food.

"Don't let them take the food," he said. "They are weak. We can take them down."

Two of the men lunged at me. Embarrassingly, I screeched.

I was terrified. I shouldn't be here, I thought. I should be at home, painting my nails and texting friends on my phone – or whatever it was I usually did. Not fighting a bunch of guys! I panicked and swung my stick at them. The stick hit one of the guys on the side of his head and he simply crumpled to the ground.

My mind registered what happened with some surprise – I did that?

Then my hands started moving on their own. I twirled the stick smoothly and shot off a stunningly fast blow to the other guy. I hit him right in the middle of his chest with the end of the stick and he dropped on the floor, gasping for breath. I stared at the poor guy in shock.

What did I just do? How did I do that? I looked over at Jae. He was surrounded by five of them while three others – including Tattoo Guy – simply stood by, watching. When they realised that I had taken down two of their guys, the three of them surged towards me.

I screamed again and panicked. This time, my wits seemed to have left me and I found myself swinging my stick wildly. Tattoo Guy easily smacked my stick away and caught my arm. In his other hand, he had a knife.

I shrieked. "Jae! Help me!"

Jae had problems of his own. He was fending off five men. I saw him take a hard blow to his stomach.

Suddenly, I felt a sharp pain shoot up my left arm, followed by something warm. I lifted my arm and saw blood.

CHAPTER 14.

I was bleeding! Tattoo Guy had slashed me!
I wrenched my arm out of his grasp and tried to
slap him. How stupid was that?

I felt my body go numb with terror as the
three men closed in on me. My arm was hurting
really badly and I felt tears threatening to spill
out at the corner of my eyes. Tattoo Guy was
watching me with a really mean look. He started
to laugh.

"Think you're so tough now, little girl?"

Little girl? Who did he think he was, calling
me little girl? Now I was angry. I felt a sensation
prickling at the back of my skull. It was a strange
but not unpleasant feeling. A series of images
appeared in my mind, like a video clip played on
high speed. I saw Tattoo Guy charge at me and
knock me to the ground with his shoulder.

I shook my head in confusion. Tattoo Guy
was still in front of me – not moving, but I could
tell he was going to. In my peripheral vision,
I saw my stick on the floor. I inched closer to it,
all the time watching him closely as he started
to move.

When he started to charge at me, I dove
towards my stick. I grabbed it in my right hand,
tucked my head to my chest and executed a

perfect roll on the floor, landing back up on my feet.

With quick reflexes I didn't know I had, I then swung the stick at his legs. He tripped and fell flat on his face, arms and legs splayed in all directions. If I hadn't been scared to death, I might actually have laughed.

When Tattoo Guy's two friends came at me, I fought like a maniac, hitting everything that came my way with the stick. I let instincts take over. My arms and legs seemed to be moving on their own. One second I was sweeping the stick at one assailant's knee, the next second, I was pivoting on the spot, my leg flying up in a kick that sent the other man backwards. Wow, that was cool, I thought.

Just when I thought it was over, there was Tattoo Guy again. And, boy, was he mad. Why wouldn't he leave me alone? It was really frustrating because I really didn't want to fight. I just wanted to go home! But he was tough and wouldn't stay down.

Then he said something that sent a chill down my spine, "You think you can just come back here and steal from me again?"

Again? Again? This man knows me? I faltered for one second. Seeing me hesitate, he launched a fierce punch at my face. Weirdly, again, I saw the whole attack play out in my mind before it actually happened. I felt that same prickling feeling. The same strange sensation...

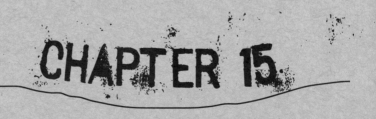

CHAPTER 15.

Which was why I was able to bring my stick up to deflect his blow. I heard a sickening crack. I think I broke his arm. I didn't feel bad. He pretty much deserved it.

He charged at me – for the third time – but I was strangely calm as I watched him. I ducked under his clumsy attack and brought my knee up to his stomach. He fell with a dull thud.

"What do you mean 'again'?" I shouted at him. "How do you know me? Who am I? Who am I?"

"Zee!" I heard Jae call out. "Behind you!"

I swung around to see three more men advancing towards me. I noted smugly that the men had abandoned their attack on Jae to deal with me. Obviously, they thought I was the bigger threat, not him. Ha! Who was the girl now?

I spun the stick in my hands calmly, then swung it at the man nearest to me. There was a satisfying crack as he took the hit on his head. He fell.

I looked at the other two men. These two looked seriously pathetic. They were so thin I could see their shoulder bones poking out from their T-shirts.

"Who's next?" I said, feeling much braver than I had at the start of the fight.

They both ran at me – one from the left and one from the right. This time, when I felt that funny sensation, I just went with it. I saw what they intended to do. One of them meant to get his arm around my neck in a chokehold. The other one, I realised with a chill, wanted to kill me.

I did the only logical thing – I simply jumped out of the way and they crashed into each other and fell onto the floor. They struggled to get up, but were so weak they slumped on the floor again.

I ran over to Jae. I think he was laughing – or trying not to. In any case, he was failing horribly.

"What's so damn funny? You could have helped me, you know!"

"Did you see their expressions?" Jae said, excited the way only a boy could get over a fight.

"Obviously not. I was too busy trying not to get killed!" I shook my head in exasperation. "What happened to the rest of them?"

Jae grinned cheekily at me. "They ran off after seeing what the evil stick-twirling monster could do."

I rolled my eyes but at the same time, felt relieved that I didn't have to fight any more crazed adults.

"And when were you going to tell me that you could fight like that? I've never seen anything like that," Jae demanded, frowning at me.

"How could I have told you if I didn't know? I didn't know..." I faltered.

Where had I learned to fight like that? And what about that thing I had felt in my head? I knew what those men were going to do. I could read their minds!

"We'd better go. In case they have a second back-up or something," Jae said, not looking at me.

I didn't need to be told a second time. I was so ready to go home. We picked up our stash of food and ran.

I wondered if I should tell Jae about what Tattoo Guy had said. I wished I had gotten him to tell me more. He might know something about who I was. And what about the weird mind-reading thing? Should I tell Jae about that, too? I bet he already thought I was weird – what would he make of this, I wondered.

I would tell him when we got back home, I decided. Our home was only about two kilometres away. We should be back in less than 20 minutes, I thought.

Boy, was I wrong.

In the end, we took something like two hours to get home. I mean, seriously.

We were crossing a big open road, away from the cluster of HDB blocks we had come from when we spotted them. Another gang of adults.

Not again!

CHAPTER 16

We ran back towards the blocks and hid behind one of the big pillars in a void deck.

"Did they see us?" I asked. I couldn't run anymore. I was ready to give up the food we had found and just go home already. All this fighting and running was too much for me.

"I don't think so," Jae said, still not looking at me.

"What are they doing?" I asked. I slumped down on the floor and used the bag of food as a back rest.

"Something's wrong," Jae said. "Take a look."

"Don't want to," I said. "Too tired."

"I'm serious. You got to look at this." His voice trembled slightly.

That got my attention. I followed his gaze.

There were about 10 of them and they were walking in a really weird way – half limping, half shuffling along. It made my stomach feel a little bit sick to see them.

"What is wrong with them?" I whispered to Jae, unable to tear my eyes away from them.

"I don't know. I've never seen adults look so bad before. Mostly, they look hungry, and they are aggressive. But this group looks different," he said.

"They are giving me the creeps," I said, shuddering.

"Then will you be quiet? I don't want them coming after us. I'm too tired to fight again," Jae scolded.

Just then, one of them – a woman – turned her head and looked right at us. I managed to stifle a scream. Jae reached for my hand and squeezed it weakly, and I was thankful I was not alone. She could not see us, of course. We were well hidden behind the pillar and a pile of old boxes, but we could see her by peering through a crack.

She started dragging her feet towards us. I watched in horror as she took one shambling step after another. As she got closer, I could see that her skin was blistered and broken. Disgusting pus-filled sores covered her arms and legs and even her face. Her hair was long and tangled and if she wasn't this pus-filled sores person, I think that she would, actually, have been quite pretty.

There was a dull empty look in her eyes as she stumbled towards us. I looked at her feet. No shoes. Her feet were covered with cuts, some not properly healed because she was leaving a trail of

pus and blood behind her as she shuffled towards
us. I was filled with terror. I turned to run, but
Jae held me firmly by the waist.

"Shh!" he whispered. "If we run, we'll be seen."

I don't know what would have happened if the
commotion hadn't broken out behind her. She
whipped her head to look and started shambling
away. We squinted from behind the boxes, trying
to make out what was going on. And then,
immediately, we wished we hadn't.

One of the adults had collapsed in the middle
of the road. Well, it looked like a man, but we
couldn't tell. The rest of the group shambled
frantically towards him. I thought they were
going to help him up.

They didn't. They didn't! Oh my God,
they didn't!

They did something else. Something
much worse. They stooped down and started
taking bites out of him.

I felt bile rising up my throat and I turned
around and threw up.

Jae looked as if he might vomit too, but
instead, he patted my back gently. My own terror,
horror and disgust were all reflected on his face.
He peered through the boxes nervously, then

looked back at me. His face was pale.

"Please be quiet," he begged as I started to cry.

He held me close to him as we huddled behind those boxes. We could not – did not – want to look anymore. After a while, the grunting and feeding sounds stopped and Jae got up to take a cautious peek. They were gone, and so was the body. They must have eaten all of him and dragged his bones away. The poor man, I thought, he was being eaten alive.

We sat there for a long time, too frightened to move away from our hiding place. What if they were still out there waiting to pounce on us?

Jae looked pale and distressed, all the bravado and swagger gone. I didn't realise I was shivering until he started to rub my back.

"It's okay. They are gone," he said, uncharacteristically gentle.

His green eyes looked right into my heart, and for no reason at all, I felt better. I gave him a weak smile. He put his arm around me and I leaned on him. It was nice.

Finally, after a long while, Jae stood up.

"Let's go. This is ridiculous. We can't sit here forever," he said.

I shook my head.

"This isn't safe either," he insisted.

He stuck his hand out. I took it and hauled my butt off the ground.

Jae took one last look to ascertain that no one was around. Still holding my hand, we ran all the way home, fuelled by the adrenalin, fear and terror coursing through our bodies.

When we finally reached our home, it was dark. Our bags of food were gone. Goodness knows where they were. We must have dropped them while we were running. Jae looked at me nervously as the kids circled us.

CHAPTER 17

"What happened to the both of you?" Shulin demanded anxiously.

"What's wrong?"

"Are you okay?"

"Where's the food?"

Everyone was jostling around us, hurling questions, fear and anxiety written all over their faces.

"We are not okay. We saw some adults. They were gross looking... very gruesome. And... and we saw them eat their own friend! " I blurted out shakily.

"He was still alive!" Jae added.

The kids recoiled in disbelief. "What? They were eating each other?"

"Where were they? What did they look like?" Kyl asked, shushing the rest of the kids with an authoritative wave.

I gave him a blank stare. My mind had shut down.

Jae was the one who answered.

"They were over by the main road, you know, near the start of the HDB estate. They looked... they looked... like zombies."

Someone laughed. I turned my head to glare. It was Dyanne.

"Zombies? Zombies? Like dead people come back to life? Oh please! Have you been watching

too many zombie movies? They went out of fashion, oh, like 10 years ago, you know."

"Yeah! Are you sure?" a frightened kid spoke up. "Maybe you were too far away. Maybe they were eating something else."

"That's right!" said Dyanne. "There's nothing to worry about."

A few other kids nodded hopefully.

Jae spoke up again, "Listen, guys. We were near enough to see them clearly. Okay, they may not be zombies, but they definitely don't look human. Something's happened to them, and we need to find out what. We need to find out if they are a danger to us."

"What do you mean?" Kyl said. "You think they can attack us?"

"Yes, I think so. One of them almost spotted us. I don't know what would have happened if she had found us," Jae said.

Suddenly, he turned his gaze on me, probably wondering why I was being so quiet. "Umm... are you okay? Oh no, there's blood running down your arm."

I touched my arm, and sure enough, I felt something hot, wet and sticky. I stared at my left arm. The cut inflicted by Tattoo Guy was still raw and angry-looking.

Suddenly, it all became too much for me. I pushed past the kids, and ran towards the back of the house. In my dazed state, I could hear Jae scrambling after me, and the kids shouting and arguing over what to do about the adult problem.

When Jae caught up with me, he touched my arm gently. "Are you okay?"

I nodded, still traumatised.

Suddenly, he pulled me into a tight hug. I stiffened, not expecting it. Then I relaxed and rested my head on his chest, taking in the warmth of his embrace and the feel of muscle under his shirt. He rubbed my back softly and said, "It'll be fine. Don't cry, okay?"

I nodded, my chest tightening. I fought back my tears.

"I've never seen them like that before. They were never this bad," Jae told me, somehow managing to run his fingers through my long tangled hair.

I nodded again, still unable to talk, but this time, for a different reason. I was acutely aware of his hand around my back and his breath on the back of my neck. I didn't want to ruin the moment.

Jae stroked my hair until I relaxed completely. Slowly, I pulled myself away and smiled at him awkwardly. "I'm okay now, thank you."

Jae took an old rag out of his pocket and pressed it to my arm. The cut wasn't very deep, but it hurt like anything. I hoped the rag was clean.

I winced. "Ouch!"

CHAPTER 18

His deep green eyes stared intently into mine as he held my injured arm. My heart beat a little faster. What was I doing? I thought. This wasn't a time to be crushing on some boy I just met!

He led me to the toilet, dipped the rag into the pail of water and put it on my arm. I held it there while he rooted around the toilet cabinets for a bandage. He found a plaster and positioned it gently on my arm.

"C'mon, apple blossom, let's get out of this stink hole," he said, trying to cheer me up.

Apple blossom? I rolled my eyes.

We walked out into the backyard and slumped on the stinky sofa. When he put his arm around me, I didn't complain.

Then out of the blue, he bolted out from the seat, bent over and threw up. He clutched his bandaged arm, his face now pale.

I looked at his arm, my eyes widening with concern. I saw a bead of blood snaking down from his bandage.

"Gosh..." I whispered. I felt so wretched. I was so wrapped up in my own misery and pain that I hadn't even stopped to consider that Jae might be in pain too. He had not once

complained about his already injured arm. The fighting must have made it worse.

"Sit back," I ordered him. Now it was my turn to take charge.

The wound, I saw, had not been cleaned properly. It was all swollen and looked infected. Yellowish pus was oozing from the long gash that stretched from his upper arm all the way down to his elbow.

I resisted the urge to gag. Running back into the toilet, I brought out the pail of water. I scooped some and poured it on Jae's arm. He bit his bottom lip and scrunched up his eyes. He looked so cute when he did that, I thought. I mentally slapped myself. Stop doing that! But I couldn't help it. There was just something about him that drew me to him.

I wiped all the blood and pus away, then wrapped his arm with a new bandage. I hoped it was enough.

He sighed and sat back. I settled down next to him, careful not to jolt his arm. We sat there in silence. It was nice.

"Tell me something, Zee," Jae said, his face regaining some normal colour. "Where did you learn how to fight like that? You were awesome."

He was looking at me strangely, with a mix of curiosity and suspicion. I sighed inwardly. Trust a boy to spoil a perfectly sweet moment!

CHAPTER 19

I looked away. "Don't look at me like that. You're freaking me out."

"I'm freaking you out?" he said incredulously. "You fight like some martial arts expert and I'm freaking you out? How about you freaking me out? Who are you, anyway?"

"Good question. I wish I knew!" I snapped, my irritation rising. I wished everyone would stop asking me who I was. If I knew, wouldn't I tell them?

"Can't you try to remember anything? Where did you live? Were you rich? Did you have brothers? Sisters?" Jae asked.

"To answer your questions: No. I don't know. I don't know. I don't know. I don't know!" I said, my voice rising to a screech.

"Some of the other kids are wondering how you managed to survive on your own for so long," Jae continued relentlessly. "And why you are so healthy. You look well fed."

I was stumped. I had no answer to that. How had I survived?

"We think that maybe there are other groups of kids like us around Singapore, surviving just like us. It would make a lot of sense," Jae said. "But in the last two months, you are the first kid we have seen around here. Maybe you are a new reject."

"What? A new what?" I said, really annoyed now. Did he just call me a reject?

"A reject. You know, thrown out of Camp Zero."

"Thrown out?" My mind was whirling again. There was too much information to process.

"Didn't you understand what we were telling you?"

"No, all I know about Camp Zero is that the people inside were specially selected. They have food and water and beds and everything. Right?"

"Yes, that's right."

"So... you mean I could have once been inside? And I was thrown out?"

"Yes."

"I don't understand. Why would they throw me out? Was my whole family thrown out?"

Jae looked at me blankly. "No. They only threw the kids out."

"Who's 'they'?"

"The adults on the inside," he said simply.

"You mean your own parents threw you out?" I asked, horrified. But at the back of my mind, I felt the hint of a memory coming back to me. An image of someone screaming flashed in my mind. I felt a wave of terror wash over me, brought on by a memory I could not grasp.

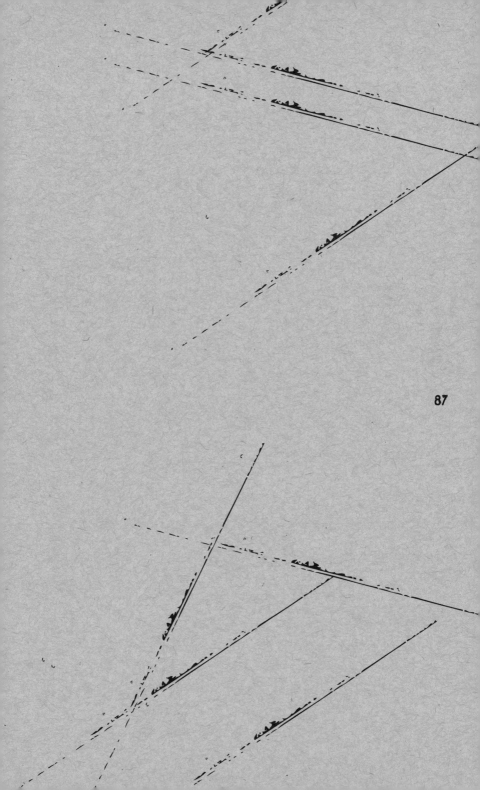

87

I closed my eyes and tried to concentrate. Something was familiar; what was it? The idea of being thrown out by adults and soldiers, it triggered a memory. But it was too far away and too fleeting. The more I tried to catch hold of it, the more it faded. I opened my eyes and urged Jae to continue.

CHAPTER 20

"They must have realised that they were not going to have enough food. So they threw us out. We never knew what was going on, and..." Jae faltered.

"I'm not sure if our parents knew what was happening, but surely they must have been told. One day, a group of soldiers just led us out. They gave us a name – Rovers – and we were all really excited. We thought it was a game, and we were so pumped up because it was getting boring in Camp Zero. Then, they left us around here. They never came back."

"What?" I said dumbly. "That's not possible. They couldn't have done that."

"It is. And they did," Jae said. "They led us out and left us to starve. Like Hansel and Gretel."

I stared at Jae. Something about what he said rang true. We had been left to die. Only this wasn't a fairy tale. This was real. We didn't have stones. And we didn't have breadcrumbs. If we did, we would probably have eaten them. And it didn't look like our happily-ever-after was anywhere near.

"So, that means that I could have just been released from Camp Zero?"

"That's what we think. It would explain a lot. We just have to figure out why you were left alone, and why you have no memory."

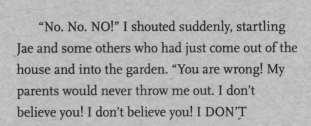

"No. No. NO!" I shouted suddenly, startling Jae and some others who had just come out of the house and into the garden. "You are wrong! My parents would never throw me out. I don't believe you! I don't believe you! I DON'T BELIEVE YOU!"

"Zee," he said calmly. "It is true. Whether you want to believe me or not is a different story altogether."

I glared at him. He looked so calm and it annoyed me.

"You're stupid!" I yelled. "Don't tell me things and expect me to believe you. I don't even know you. You don't know me."

At the back of my mind, a little voice warned me not to continue down this path. Don't rant like a crazy person again, the little voice told me. You actually like his attention, it said. But I pushed the thought away angrily. I stood up and faced Jae.

"I don't want to talk to you anymore. GO AWAY!"

I was now shouting hysterically. The events of the past two days had caught up with me. Waking up with no memory of who I was, to a world I didn't remember. Being set upon by thugs and having to fight them off. Discovering that I could read minds. Coming across crazed man-eating adults. And now, being told that my parents had plotted to abandon me – to save themselves. It was all too much.

I pushed past the gaping kids and ran into the house. I ran blindly, opened the first door I came across, flung myself in and locked the door behind me. Luckily for me, it was a nice little room with no windows, so no one could see me make a fool of myself, crying like a baby.

So, that is my story thus far... at least the last two days that I can remember. I don't know who I am. I don't know where I came from. All I know is I am here now, stuck in this room, in this house full of kids who think I'm a freak.

I'M NOT GOING TO DIE HERE.
AND WHILE I STILL CAN,

I WILL
FIGHT TO
SURVIVE.

When I wake up the next day, I am stiff and sore all over. Jae is standing over me with a sympathetic grin on his face.

"Hey, are you awake?" he asks, an embarrassed smile on his face.

CHAPTER 21

I look around. I am still in the little room, lying on the floor. I must have cried myself to sleep. How pathetic. My mouth feels icky and dry and I simply grunt at Jae and try to shoo him away. He refuses to go.

"Are you okay? I'm really sorry I upset you yesterday. We've been living like this for more than two months, and we've all kind of accepted the fact that we were left to die. It must have been a shock for you to find out the way you did. I'm really sorry," he says. He reaches his hand out, offering to pull me up.

I ignore him, still feeling sore, tired and grumpy. And guess what? I still can't remember anything. I sigh inwardly. Then it occurs to me that I locked the door yesterday.

"Hey, how did you get in here anyway? I locked the door!" I demand in a voice that sounds disgustingly raspy.

"Uh... I can pick locks, remember? I opened this door in, like, two seconds," Jae says, a tad smugly.

"So why didn't you come get me earlier? You just left me here the whole night?"

"Err... umm, I thought you wanted some privacy."

I glare at him coldly. I'm angry. Not at him, particularly, but just angry. I'm in such a bad mood I want to lash out at somebody, anybody, but I hold myself back. These kids have only been trying to help me. Jae has been nothing but patient with me. Plus, right now, he looks so cute standing there looking sheepish. I feel my anger seeping away a little and I offer a weak smile.

"C'mon, let's get you some water and get you cleaned up. You'll feel much better, I promise," he says, offering his hand again. This time, I take it and he hauls me up and pushes me out the door. So much for male chivalry.

After a dismal breakfast of dry crackers – only two each – Kyl gathers us all and makes an announcement.

"Jae and I have decided that we need to start planning again. We have been too complacent for the past four weeks, living in this house," he begins. "We need to really go out to look for more food every day. We need to be more organised. We need to be able to pack up and run if we need to. We've been a little too comfortable here."

"Comfortable? You call this comfortable?" a boy shouts out.

"You know what I mean," Kyl continues,

putting his hands up to shush the kids. "I know the first few weeks were really hard. We had nothing, we had no plan. We just slept outside and ate whatever we could find. After finding this house with all this food, we've become a little lazy. This food is not going to last forever. Jae and I looked at the store. I think we have food to last us all for maybe three weeks – four, if we are really careful. What are we going to do after that? We need to start planning now."

I look around and notice some kids nodding in agreement. A few of them look really depressed.

"What's the use?" Dyanne says. "We are all going to die anyway. We might as well just eat all the food now and die happy."

The kids stare at her in shock, but I can tell that her words have hit home with some of them. I myself can't help but wonder if she is right. Are we all doomed to die? If there is no food left, isn't death a certainty? Why delay the inevitable?

It is Brion who breaks the silence. "I don't know about you, but I'm not giving up that easily. I'm not going to die here. And while I still can, I'm going to fight to survive. We are still alive, aren't we? I don't think anyone expected us to live, but we are still here. I don't intend to give up now."

CHAPTER 22

"Exactly," Kyl says. "We need to fight. We need to survive. And we need a plan."

"Don't forget, we have a new threat. Those crazy adults we saw yesterday. We need to form a team to check them out. We need to know how many of them there are, and whether they are dangerous," Jae adds.

Before Dyanne can retort, a loud crashing sound coming from the front door startles us. I grab a stick. I don't know what else to do. Together with Jae and some older kids, I rush towards the front just as someone barges in from the living room.

It is the man from yesterday. Tattoo Guy! He is wearing a different shirt, but I would recognise those tattoos anywhere, not to mention his bald head. How did he find us? I was sure we weren't followed.

He blusters into our dining room. He scans the crowd of faces and stops at mine.

"You!" he screams. His neck muscles are bulging with exertion and he looks furious. "Give me back my food!"

In all the excitement yesterday, I had forgotten to tell Jae and the other kids that Tattoo Guy had recognised me, and that he might somehow know me. I don't feel like telling them now, seeing as how I seem to have led the guy right to their hideout.

Jae, quite needlessly, jumps to my rescue. "It is not your food. We found it ourselves. Go find your own food."

"I can handle this," I whisper to Jae. "Back off."

That prickling sensation is creeping up on me and I know that Tattoo Guy is about to attack. He runs at us and I see everything he intends to do. He wants to charge at me and push me down. Really? That's all he can come up with?

I swing my stick, catching his ankles and making him stumble. He is up again in a flash and I panic. He swings at me and catches me just under my chin with his fist. Oww! That hurts and I stumble backwards into Jae. He holds me steady and then jumps in front of me, shielding me. The other kids are simply too shocked to do anything but stare. I notice that many are backing up the staircase.

I take a quick breath and tell myself to calm down. That's when I see what happens next. Tattoo Guy has been hiding a knife in his back pocket and the flashing images in my mind show me that he will throw it at Jae, but I'm ready for him. I take a small step to the left of Jae and brace myself.

Jae is completely oblivious to the danger he is in. His hands are outstretched – the idiot is unwittingly presenting his body as a target – and he's taunting Tattoo Guy. "C'mon, big guy. Think you can come here and beat up my kids?"

His kids? Since when were we his kids? But no one argues with this.

Tattoo Guy reaches behind his back and the knife comes hurtling right at Jae. He has moved so fast Jae doesn't have time to react. But I do. With a quick calculated flick, my stick connects with the airborne knife. The impact knocks the knife off-course and it heads up, towards the ceiling.

I watch the knife fly upwards, then start to fall back down. My hands twirl the stick. It spins, and for a moment, I feel like a cheerleader with a baton. Another flick and the stick connects with the knife again, sending it right at Tattoo Guy's feet. He jumps away just in time and the knife spins away, hitting the wall behind him.

Jae and Tattoo Guy gape at me in shock.

I swing the stick again, catching him in the stomach, making him double over. He is beaten and he knows it. He turns around and scrambles out the way he came in.

"Ha! That showed you!" I yell after him. "Don't come back!"

Then I see Jae, still gaping at me. "What just happened? How did you know what he was going to do?"

All the other kids are staring too. Some in admiration, some in fear. But mostly in shock. I look at my hands and realise I am trembling. How am I going to explain something I don't understand myself?

"I'll tell you later. We need to move," I say, swiftly changing the subject. "If Tattoo Guy found us, it means his friends must know where we are. We need to go... Now!"

Somehow, we manage to round up all the kids to make plans. I guess one good thing has come out of Tattoo Guy's attack – it has galvanised us all into action. Because, like it or not, our cosy hideout has been discovered. Staying is not an option.

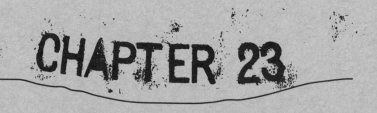

CHAPTER 23

Even Dyanne has stopped being sulky and is in take-charge mode. As I look over at her, she is comforting some of the younger children, all the while barking orders to others. I am tasked with the fairly easy job of sorting food into bags – one for each of us to carry.

I listlessly stuff food into bags, in no particular order, and paying no attention to whether the food is being divided equally among the bags. I feel my mind shutting down again, going numb. Please, please let this be some terrible dream, I hope.

I must have fallen asleep – seriously, can you blame me after everything I have gone through in the last few days? – because the next thing I know, I feel someone shaking my shoulders. It is Dyanne and she is yelling something. I am so fatigued I don't even bother to get up. I lie in my nest of cartons, scattered tins and assorted packets of dried food.

"What the hell do you think you are doing?"

"I'm tired. I must have dozed off. Geez, calm down," I mutter.

"Here we are, working like crazy, and you find the time to take a nap?"

She kicks the bag at my feet and continues barking, "Are you even packing these bags correctly?"

"There is a right way to pack bags?"
I ask lamely.

"Of course there is!" she screeches.

She pours out the entire contents of two bags.
"You put all the canned food into two bags? Who
do you think is strong enough to carry them? Don't
you have any brains? Divide the cans equally into
all the bags so that we all share the weight. Then
divide up all the rest of the dried food. Every bag
should contain some biscuits, some instant noodles
and some rice. So that if we get separated from one
another, we have enough to survive on our own."

"Oh." How am I supposed to know that? It
isn't every day that I am tasked with packing a
survival bag!

Thankfully, Kyl comes to my rescue.

"What's going on in here?" he says.

Dyanne rolls her eyes. "Your little charity
project is making a mess of the food. What a
waste of time. Some help she's turned out to be!"

She storms out of the pantry, where I am still
sprawled pathetically.

"C'mon," he says gently. "Let's get this done.
We're running out of time."

We work till eight in the evening. It has
taken us an entire day to get everything

organised. They have obviously done this before. Everyone has done his bit – no fuss, no arguing. The younger kids automatically look up to the older kids for leadership and simply do what they are told to do. I feel a strange pride that they are handling themselves so well.

Each of us has two bags to carry. One for essentials like extra clothes, a set of cutlery, a lighter, a bottle of water, candles and a blanket and another – thanks to me – neatly packed with food. Despite my efforts to stuff each bag with as much food as I can, there is still a fair amount of food left in the pantry – two cartons of sardines and three sacks of rice.

As much as we hate to leave so much food behind, there is no way for us to lug the rice around with us. In the end, we decide to hide the food in a small dried-out fish pond in the front garden. We carefully wrap the food with waterproof garbage bags and cover the whole lot with rocks and soil. When we run out of food, we can come back to this secret stash.

I tap Jae's shoulder. "We should move. Tattoo Guy will be back."

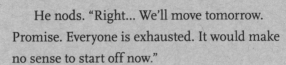

He nods. "Right... We'll move tomorrow. Promise. Everyone is exhausted. It would make no sense to start off now."

Also, he doesn't mention the obvious question hanging in the air – where are we going to go?

"Fine," I say. "Good night."

We are all feeling too vulnerable to be separated, so we all huddle together on the floor in the living room. Everyone falls asleep quickly – everyone, that is, except me. Maybe my earlier nap has refreshed me, maybe I am nervous. Whatever the reason, my mind keeps churning.

Who am I? What happened to me? Why is this happening to me? How can this be real? Why can't I remember? Did I really get abandoned? I lie down and gaze at the stars outside the window. They glimmer with a hope I do not feel. I try to remember where I came from, who I am – everything – but everything's a blur of confusion. Misery wells up in my chest and, frustrated, I find myself crying. Again.

A scream wakes me up. Eryn points out the window. "Wha-wha-what's tha-that s-s-sound?" she stammers.

We hear strange grunting and groaning sounds coming from outside.

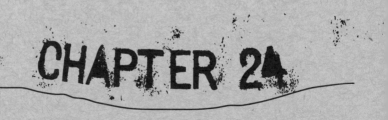

CHAPTER 24

We all run upstairs to get a better view. We spot a group of about 20 adults coming down the street towards our house. They are about 10 houses away. I recognise their strange shambling, shuffling way of moving.

"It's them," I say simply. "The weird adults we saw."

"You mean the Eaters?" a little boy next to me asks.

The Eaters? Yes, that's a good word for them.

"Yes, the Eaters," I say.

"They look funny," Brion says.

Dyanne is the first to react. She starts giving instructions and I am suddenly glad for her bossiness.

"Everyone, grab your packs! We have to go now! We have to run!"

Everyone rushes around madly, and I take one last look outside. The Eaters are making weird grunting noises and crashing through everything in their path. Most of them are stumbling forward blindly, mindlessly. There are a few that look more alert, who turn their heads from side to side.

I see one woman Eater fall, but none of them bothers to try to help her up. They just walk over her. She screeches in pain. One of the Eaters turns back and starts towards her. He bends over and reaches for her hand. He takes a bite. More follow suit and the screams of the woman Eater get louder. I turn away and shoo the younger kids away from the window. I shudder.

They are getting closer and closer. We hear a dull thud coming from the front door. We all run down the stairs and through the kitchen. We spill out the back door into the garden at the back of the house.

"They are coming!" one of the younger girls screams.

The pounding on the front door gets louder. The strange grunting takes on an urgent quality. A chill runs down my spine. I am terrified. More kids scream.

"What do we do now?" I grab Jae's arm in panic.

"We need to get out of here," Jae says.

Jae and Kyl run to a small metal gate in the wall surrounding the garden. It leads out to a storm drain running along the back of all the houses on this street. There is a narrow ledge along the drain. We can escape from there!

Brion runs to help them, but the metal gate is jammed. It won't even budge.

Kyl tries to push the gate open but it is wedged firmly in its place. I hear a loud thud and a crash. The front door has fallen. Jae and I hit the gate with Kyl.

"Over. We need to go over the wall," Brion says.

I look around at the frightened faces. There are 15 of us. How will we get over in time? The wall is so tall, over two metres high. What are we going to do?

"The sofa!" I yell. "Drag the sofa here!"

Jae and Kyl drag the sofa over to the wall. Standing on the back of the sofa, Kyl easily reaches the top of the wall. He clambers up and sits astride the top of the wall. Jae is pushing the little kids up to Kyl, who grabs them by their arms and hauls them over. They all look terrified, but they're being so brave.

I hear a shriek. "They're coming!"

We are not going to be able to get all the kids over the wall in time. Brion and I pound harder against the gate in the wall but to no avail. The grunting noises are getting nearer. They are definitely in the house.

I turn to look back and see that the door leading out to the backyard is open. I see a whole group of Eaters swarm into the kitchen. Dyanne and Brion stand guard over the younger kids, getting ready to defend them.

I run back towards the house. I grab the door handle and slam the door shut. It seems a silly and futile gesture, seeing as the door locks from the inside. I pull back the door with every ounce of strength I can muster.

Dyanne runs to help me. I feel a tug on the other side and the door starts to open.

"Hurry up!" Dyanne shouts to Kyl and Jae. "We can't keep this up much longer!"

The door opens a crack and a hand worms its way into the gap. It is blistered, bloody and totally disgusting. The hand grips the door, yanking and pulling.

"What do we do?!" I gasp at Dyanne.

"Pull on three!" she shouts. "One... two... THREE!"

We pull the door shut. Something falls on the floor at my feet. I look down. It is a finger. I shudder.

Dyanne and I look at each other in disgust as it twitches on the floor.

"Jae! Kyl! Anybody! Help!" I scream.

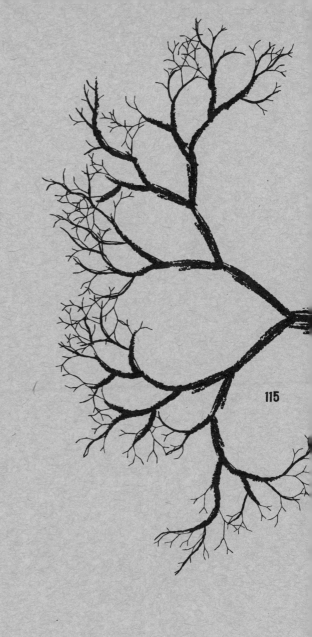

115

Brion runs over
and grabs the door
handle. It seems
to work. The door
remains closed. The
pounding coming
from the other side
rattles the door.
I am so terrified I
want to scream.

CHAPTER 25

I look over at the back wall. Jae and Kyl are still hauling kids over. Five kids left. Plus me, Brion and Dyanne. I am relieved to note that Eryn isn't in the garden anymore. She must be on the other side of the wall. Now, four kids left.

Just when I start to think that we just might be able to make it, the pounding stops. Something doesn't feel right. It's too quiet.

Then there is a huge crack and a fist comes through the wooden door, barely missing my head. I scream and let go. Brion and Dyanne desperately hang on to the door handle. I look around, panting in fear.

That familiar tingling feeling creeps up my neck. It takes me a split second to realise that I need to see what's coming. I freeze and concentrate. The tingling stops. No!!

The fist comes through the door again and another surge of fear shoots through me when Dyanne lets the door handle go with a scream. There is only Brion holding the door in place. Skinny geeky Brion is the only thing between us and them. The Eaters.

The tingling sensation starts again, this time, from my forehead and around my eyes. It makes my face itch. I try to breathe. I see the flashing

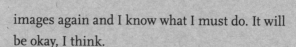

images again and I know what I must do. It will be okay, I think.

I grab Dyanne and push her towards the wall. "Go! I can handle this."

She hesitates.

"Go! Help the other kids get over!" I shout.

She runs to Jae and the three remaining kids.

"Brion, let go," I say.

"Wh-what? Are you mad?"

"Just let go, Brion. When I count to three, run to Jae. Get all the kids over and run. I will be okay. I promise," I say.

"No!"

I ignore him. "One. Two. THREE!"

I practically yank him off and shove him towards the wall. I wait. The door swings open and I am face to face with an Eater.

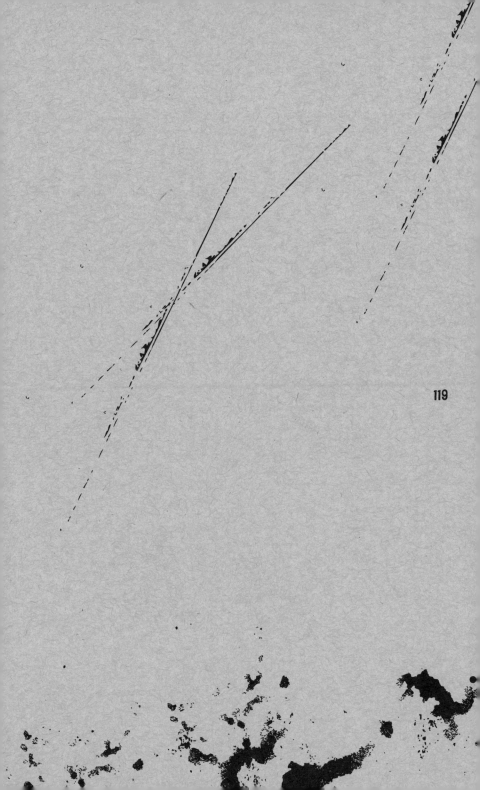

119

I don't know why, but I no longer feel fear. Behind me, Dyanne is screaming something. Jae too. I ignore them and try to keep calm. I need to focus on the images flying through my mind. Unlike when I faced Tattoo Guy and could see his thoughts, there are no thoughts I can see. Maybe they have none. But I can see what they intend to do.

CHAPTER 26

The first Eater through the door lunges at my throat, both hands out, Egyptian-mummy style.

I scowl at him. "Oh, no, you don't."

I swing my arm forward and punch him in the jaw. I hear a crack. There go my knuckles. The Eater flies backwards into several other Eaters and stays down.

My right hand is throbbing. I refuse to look at it, afraid of what I will see. I grab a laundry pole off a nearby stack with my left hand and swing it lightly, testing its weight. As I shift it to my right hand, a pain flares though my arm. I almost drop the stick. I clench my teeth, push the pain into a box and lock it. That's for me to think about later.

Two more Eaters come at me. I brace myself. I let my mind relax and let my instincts take over. My left arm – still slightly wounded – bears the weight of the pole as I swing it sideways and around my head, gaining momentum as it comes back round. I hit them both on their heads and the two Eaters drop like puppets with their strings cut.

Two more rush out. These are women. Or were women. I don't know what they are now. One of them doesn't even have eyes, just gaping sockets. I take her – or it – down first with a quick flick to her knees. She keels over and stays down. I twirl the pole as my body turns and score a hit on the other Eater and she goes down too. It is very strange. They don't look dead, but those that get knocked down don't seem able to get up.

I'm tired, but the adults are relentless. They keep coming. And coming. And coming. The next wave sees three more come at me. These are men and they look bigger. I take a few steps back, luring them into the backyard where I have more space to move.

"Zee!" Jae is shouting.

"Go, I'm fine," I say. And really, I am. I know the ending of this story, because I have seen it in my mind. It is a happy ending. For me. Not so much for the Eaters.

I wait as they shamble towards me. I see the one in the front eye me with a sly look. He looks different. Maybe he's not gone totally Eater yet. He stumbles.

"Get him!" Kyl yells from the top of the wall.

I get distracted and glance back at him. Only one child left. Good! After this, just Dyanne and Jae to go. Then me.

The Eater leaps up. He has been pretending to be weak. Dyanne screams. But I wasn't fooled.

I knew. I have already planted the pole firmly in the ground. Gripping the pole tightly with both hands for support, I launch both my feet right at his oncoming face. There is a sickening crunch and he, too, crumples to the ground.

The two behind him lumber forward mindlessly. Still holding on to the pole, I take one, two big running steps around it before taking off. I swing around the pole like some amazing acrobat. I allow the momentum to bring me around towards the coming Eaters. I bring my legs in, then kick out. One foot in each face.

"Zee!" Dyanne and Jae yell. They are already both halfway up the wall. Kyl is hauling them both up at once.

I yank the pole out and run towards the wall. Dyanne has already gone over. Jae is, like Kyl, sitting astride the wall, ready to pull me over. I scramble up the sofa and allow them to pull me up.

Reluctantly, I let my pole go. I reach the top and look back. Through the kitchen door, I see an entire horde of Eaters. Confused by the fallen Eaters in their path, they don't seem to know what to do.

Carefully, I stand on top of the wall. This way, I can see over the neighbouring houses.

I feel the blood drain from my face. The entire street leading up to our house is filled with Eaters. They seem to be coming down the road, straight towards us!

"You gotta see this," I say to Kyl and Jae.

Are all the adults turning into Eaters? Why is this happening? Soon, there'll be so many, we won't be able to fight them off. We'll all get eaten. I shove that thought out of my mind. Shut up! Shut up!

"We have to go!" I scream at Jae and Kyl.

More of the Eaters are taking bites out of the fallen Eaters. Others are shuffling towards us. Kyl climbs down the wall on the other side.

As I'm about to climb down too, Jae loses his balance and falls back into the backyard. He jumps up and tries to grab hold of the top of the wall. He misses.

"Jae!" I scream. I lean over and yank him up, almost tipping over. We fall over the other side ungracefully and I glance at him in relief.

The rest of the group are waiting, lined up on the narrow path along the edge of the big storm drain, not knowing which way to go.

"The Eaters are coming from that way," I say, pointing to where I have seen them. "We have to go the other way."

"Go!" Kyl shouts. "Run, run, run!"

I'm the last in line, watching everyone's backs. I hear someone else scream. Shriller and more high-pitched. It's one of the younger kids. It's coming from the other side of the wall. Who is it? How could we have left one behind?

CHAPTER 27

"Help me. Help meeee!"

"JAE!" I scream.

He runs back, a questioning look on his face. I don't have time to explain. I put my hands on his shoulders and jump up. I think I step on his stomach too. I hear him grunt and he falls backwards.

"What the...?" he shouts.

I lean over and look. It's a 10-year-old boy. I forget his name. Mikey or Mickey or Nicky? He is being grabbed by one of the adults! He's wailing hysterically, struggling and kicking with all his might.

My eyes widen in horror. In the panic, he must've have hidden somewhere and gone unnoticed. I feel my heart drop to my stomach.

His screams get more desperate as more Eaters get closer.

"Help..." he wails. "Help..."

I see my pole still leaning against the wall. I swing one leg over so I'm sitting astride the wall. I grab the pole and swing wildly and clumsily at the Eater.

I am totally panicking. What has happened to my mad skills? The boy is still stretching for the top of the wall, not quite reaching it.

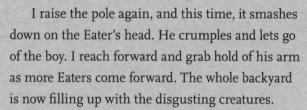

I raise the pole again, and this time, it smashes down on the Eater's head. He crumples and lets go of the boy. I reach forward and grab hold of his arm as more Eaters come forward. The whole backyard is now filling up with the disgusting creatures.

One lunges at the boy and sinks his fingernails into his arm. His skin rips apart, forming a long gash. He screams in agony. His cries seem to startle the other Eaters. Still, they stretch their arms forward, moving towards him and the smell of his blood.

The boy is visibly shaking. It angers me to see someone so young and so small get hurt.

Before another Eater gets nearer, I pull the sobbing boy up the wall and lower him to Jae on the other side.

"Hurry," I say to Jae.

Jae takes the boy gently and sets him down. The boy clings on to Jae.

"Come down. What are you waiting for?" Jae's voice is loud and urgent. His strong, gentle hands tug at my leg.

What am I waiting for? I guess I want to observe them. I am relatively safe up here. They are not smart enough to climb up the sofa. They seem oddly still, waiting.

I lean over the wall and face the Eaters.
"STAY AWAY from my kids!" I snarl.

That gets the Eaters' attention. They shamble
my way. Then, as I watch, they go still again,
waiting. I swing my pole madly, hitting the Eaters
nearer to me.

"GET AWAY! GET AWAY!" I scream.

My aim is way off and I only manage
to graze two of them, not really injuring either.
But the rest start shambling towards me again,
towards my hysterical screams.

Something clicks in my brain. Shut up, you
idiot! I tell myself. I go perfectly still and let the
pole drop. The Eaters go still and wait. So that
must be their weakness... they can't see? They
must be attracted to sound! I have to warn
the others.

I haul myself over back to Jae and the boy. Jae
is staring strangely at me, not quite angry, but not
happy either.

"It's sound," I whisper. "They are attracted to
noise. We have to warn the others."

Jae nods, understanding. The three of us
run to catch up with the rest, who are by now,
far ahead.

We run along the back alley, passing the back of the terrace houses. When we catch up with the rest of the group, we do a quick head count. All 15 are accounted for, I note with relief. I explain what I think I've learnt about the Eaters. They are attracted to sound, so we must be quiet.

CHAPTER 28

We stop when we come to the end of the path. In front of us is a main road. We have two options: up on the main road, or down into the storm drain that continues in a tunnel under the road. The main road seems deserted. The side streets running perpendicular to both sides of the main road seem empty too.

"So, up or down?" Brion asks Kyl.

Jae peers into the tunnel. It is pitch black. The boy – it turns out his name is Nicky – whimpers as he continues to cling to Jae. His arm is no longer bleeding, but the wound looks bad.

"I-I don't want to go down there," he says fearfully. "Can't we just go into a house? What about that one?"

He points to a house on the opposite side of the street. It doesn't look like it's ever been broken into. Also, it sits invitingly close.

"Or this one," he says, pointing to the house we are standing right behind. "The fence is so low, we can all just climb over."

"Please?" Eryn says.

"Please, please?" some of the other kids plead.

They are tired and their bags are heavy. Kyl's shoulders slump, and I think he's about to relent. I lean against the fence and close my eyes. I am so tired. I hope he says yes.

My eyes flick open. It's that tingly feeling, at the back of my neck. Where's the danger? Where's the danger?

"Shh! Quiet!" I put my hand out to shush the kids. The kids stare at me, wide-eyed with fear.

I push away from the fence like it's electrified and look behind me. I peer through the gaps in the fence. Kyl and Jae do the same. There is nothing in the backyard.

"What's going on?" Jae asks me.

Now is not the time to explain to him how, when I get a tingly sensation, it signals danger. And how I can see things in my mind and read people's thoughts. He just has to trust me. I signal to everyone to keep quiet, and to stay down. They all obey immediately. Except Jae. He stays stubbornly next to me. I feel both relieved and annoyed.

"What is it?" Jae whispers.

"I sense something nearby," I say softly.

"Like Spiderman, spidey-sense?" he whispers, smiling.

I don't understand how he can joke at a time like this. Then, I see the fear in his eyes and I understand that he's putting on a brave face for the younger kids. I, too, smile.

"Yeah, like Spiderman," I say.

The images start. One after another, I see flickering images in my mind. What I see fills me with dread. They are in the tunnel. The Eaters. A whole horde of Eaters shuffling, shuffling, shuffling nearer.

Jae sees the look on my face and grabs my hand and pulls me to him.

"Tell me now," he whispers fiercely into my ear.

"They're in the tunnel," I say. "We need to move everyone. Now. Quietly."

He nods, understanding. He releases my hand and I suddenly feel lost and weak. He takes charge. He smiles widely, like everything is okay. He gestures for Kyl to come to him and he whispers something in his ear. Kyl jerks back in alarm, then nods.

"Okay, okay, you win," Kyl whispers to the group. He smiles, but I see the panic on his face. "Let's go into this house. As quietly as you can."

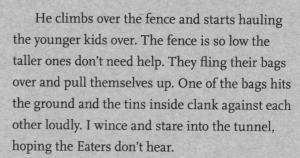

He climbs over the fence and starts hauling the younger kids over. The fence is so low the taller ones don't need help. They fling their bags over and pull themselves up. One of the bags hits the ground and the tins inside clank against each other loudly. I wince and stare into the tunnel, hoping the Eaters don't hear.

I hear a low moan. No! Tears spring to my eyes. Please, not now! I am so tired. Jae and I stare into the tunnel. I half expect an Eater to spring out at me, but nothing comes out. Jae nudges me and I realise that everyone has gone over. I jump over easily and Jae goes over last.

Everyone is waiting for him at the back door. He flashes a tired smile and gets started on picking the lock. He opens it in less than a minute.

The house smells musty and damp. We all file inside gratefully. I take one last look beyond the fence and into the tunnel and shut the door as quietly as I can.

I turn to Jae and shrug. "It could've been worse."

Exhausted, I sink to the floor with my back against the door and take stock of the situation:

1. I can't remember who I am.
2. All the plants and animals are dead.
3. We have been left to die, probably by our parents.
4. The only food we have is in our bags.
5. We have just lost our home.

Is that all? Oh, wait. I almost forgot. We are being chased by cannibals. Great. Juuuust great.

I think of all the little kids huddled up beside me shivering and wonder how their parents could've been so selfish to abandon them. What stupid parent, even if they were dying, would send their child into this hell? Not that I know what hell's like. But I'm sure it's no worse than this.

Dyanne is in take-charge mode again, and I am grateful. She moves us all into the living room and divides us into three groups of five. There are two older kids per group. Brion and I are put in charge of one group. Eryn is in my group. Her smile cheers me up. Dyanne and Shulin are in charge of another group, while Kyl and Jae take the last group.

CHAPTER 29

We should have done this a long time ago.
Then poor Nicky wouldn't have been left behind.
I look over at him. He's lying on the floor, asleep.
From exhaustion, trauma or sickness, I can't tell.
At least he's stopped whimpering.

Jae catches my attention and waves me over to
the window overlooking the backyard.

"Are you sure there are Eaters in there?" he asks,
eyeing me carefully. "Are you going to tell me what's
going on with you?"

I avoid his stare. Should I tell? Why not, I decide.
What's the worst that can happen?

"I can see things," I say.

"What do you mean?"

"Sometimes, when something bad is about to
happen, I can see it before it happens," I say.

"You saw Eaters in the storm drain?"

"Yes."

"When has this happened before?"

"Both times when the Tattoo Guy attacked us.
Also in the house just now, with the Eaters."

"If you can see danger, why didn't you warn us
before?" Jae says. He is angry. He grabs my arm
painfully. "Why?"

"It's not like I can control when I can see
things," I say, shaking his hand off.

"And your fighting skills?" he asks coldly.
"Where did that come from?"

"I don't know," I say. "I really don't."

Jae sighs. He places his hand on my back and leans towards me. He rests his forehead on my shoulder. "What am I going to do with you?"

I shrug. His head moves up and down with my shoulder. I smile at the sight. I shrug again. Up and down, up and down, until his head rolls off my shoulder. I laugh at the indignant look on his face.

"Are you going to tell the rest?" I ask.

He makes a face. "No, I'm not. It's probably better this way. For now."

He's so cute, I think.

Shut up! I stop myself, slapping my face.

Jae frowns at me and I grin sheepishly, waving my hand in front of my face. "Ahaha... Sorry, I was thinking about something." Something like your face.

I slap myself again and Jae stifles a laugh. "Are you okay, dandelion?"

Dandelion?

How many flower names can one boy think of? Well, two can play at that game.

"I'm fine, chocolate muffin." I glare at him.

I see his cheeks turn pink but I pretend I don't.

We settle down in
the new house.
I keep going back
into the backyard to
see whether there
are any Eaters. But
I guess luck is on
our side this time,
and I spot none
of them.

RUN.HIDE.SEEK

CHAPTER 30

Dyanne spends the day sorting through all our supplies, deciding on our one meal for the day. Everyone gets one can of baked beans. Yuk. But I'm too hungry to care. I scrape the bottom of my can. I check out the mound of food that we have carried with us. What will happen when that runs out? Will we, too, turn into Eaters, crazed with hunger? I push the thought away.

It's about eight, and we'll have to wake up early tomorrow. The younger kids are herded into the upstairs bedrooms.

I check all the windows and Jae relocks all the doors. Dyanne and Shulin line up all the bags, in case we need to grab them and run, like we did this morning. Then they go upstairs to tuck all the kids in.

I look in one of the rooms and I see Eryn and Brion in serious conversation. Eryn's face lights up and she throws her arms around Brion. He hesitates for a moment, his face turning a bright shade of red, and hugs her back. I turn away, smiling to myself.

I head back downstairs and lie down on the sofa in the living room that acts as my bed. I shut my eyes as I hear Jae come down and prop himself against the sofa. He reaches up and takes my hand. I smile and drift off to sleep.

"*Come on, little girl. Scared of me?*"

"*Go away,*" I shout. "*I'm not afraid of you. Go pick on someone your own size!*"

"*No way. I'm not going to let you steal from me again.*"

I jerk awake, gasping for air. Jae looks up at me sleepily.

"What'sgoingon?" he mumbles.

"I know how I'm gonna find out who I am! The Tattoo Guy! He knows me!"

Suddenly awake, Jae bolts to his feet. "Yes! He recognised you, didn't he?"

He grabs me into an unexpected hug and I just stand there in surprise, thankful for the darkness that is concealing the blush on my face.

"We should go now. Before they all wake up. I'll tell Kyl." He rushes off without giving me a chance to reply.

"Let's go," he says when he comes back. He is holding a length of rope in one hand. He slips his other hand into mine.

I realise how natural it feels and I squeeze his hand and smile up at him. Those familiar green eyes stare back at me. I wish I could remember where I had seen eyes like these before.

143

We slip out the front door. I am creeped out by the darkness. No street lamps, no light shining from people's houses, no people anywhere. The weak moonlight just about gives us enough light to see by. I wonder where the Eaters have gone. We jog back towards our old house hand in hand, looking out for Eaters and Tattoo Guy.

CHAPTER 31

I look up at the gates of our old house. They look all battered and bruised now. One of the front gates hangs off its hinges. I peer down the street but don't see anything. I shiver as a gust of wind blows against me. Jae puts his arm around my shoulder and smiles at me.

"It'll be okay," he says quietly.

We creep inside. My senses are on high alert. My imagination is going crazy and every shape I see looks like an Eater waiting to pounce on me. But there's no one there. We creep into the kitchen. There is a stench of rotting flesh. The whole place is covered with slime and I almost slip and fall. We look out into the backyard.

"There's nothing there. What happened to all the bodies? The ones I knocked down?" I ask.

"I don't think they were dead."

"They were eaten, weren't they?" Jae whispers.

"But there's nothing left. Not even bones." I shudder.

"C'mon. Let's stop freaking ourselves out," Jae says.

We go back inside and sit alone together in a corner of the living room. Waiting.

"Are you okay?" he asks.

I nod. "A little scared, I guess. You think Tattoo Guy will come? What if he's come and gone already? Or what if he came, and was caught by the Eaters? What if he's dead?"

I am stressing out. I want to know who I am. I need to know what Tattoo Guy knows about me.

He puts his arm around me and pulls me to him. I lean against him. It's nice. Except for one thing.

"You stink," I say.

"Excuse me. You don't smell so great yourself, honeysuckle," he retorts.

"Don't honeysuckle me, you pumpkin pie." Oh, I am so witty today.

"You want to play Face-Off with me? Really?" His tone is challenging.

"Why not? It's not as if you can think of anything better to do."

I give him a defiant look. I am ready for whatever insult he can hurl at me. I've got some good insults I've been crafting in my head since I saw the three of them go at each other.

"Who says I can't," he says.

He reaches out and touches my face with the back of his hand. I am not expecting this. I stare

into his green eyes. He draws my face closer to his and leans in. I feel his breath on my lips and my stomach does a thousand backflips. His lips almost brush mine.

There is a noise and we jerk apart. Someone is coming in through the front door. I hold my breath. It is Tattoo Guy. He slinks in. He can't see us but we can see him, silhouetted against the moonlight. He is alone.

"Jake! Sean! Are you here?" he whispers loudly.

"On three," Jae says, which means on one.

"One," he says, and we charge.

Tattoo Guy yells as I tackle his legs and bring him down. I hang on tight as he tries to free himself. I'm stronger than he is. Jae manages to tie his hands behind his back. He loops the rope around his legs and ties them together too. He's a much easier target than the Eaters. I grin up at Jae and he offers me a half smile.

Jae hauls Tattoo Guy into a sitting position.

"You!" he says when he sees me.

"You know me? Where do you know me from? Tell me!" I say, shaking his shoulders.

Tattoo Guy shrugs nonchalantly. And that annoys me.

I slap him. Hard.

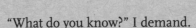

"What do you know?" I demand.

"What?"

"Why are you following me?"

"I am not following you."

"Then why are you here?"

"I want my food!"

"It isn't your food," Jae says, stepping in.

The conversation doesn't seem to be going anywhere. I storm into the kitchen and grab a cheese grater.

"I'll use this on you if you don't tell me."

"You wouldn't dare."

I narrow my eyes at him. He's right. I don't dare. I fling the grater away in frustration.

"Talk," Jae says, coming to stand next to me.

"About what?" he asks. He looks truly puzzled.

"Who am I? You recognised me!" I am so angry, but I try to keep my voice low. "Tell me who I am!"

It takes him a moment to realise what I'm asking him. He laughs. "You've lost your memory? Oh, that serves you right. I'm not telling you."

I am at a loss for words. I kick his legs, but somehow, it brings me no comfort. Kicking a tied-up man seems really mean and I can't do it again.

"Please. Just tell me who I am."

"Or else what?" he says, mocking me.

"Or else I will leave you tied up here. For the Eaters to find," Jae says.

That seems to have an effect on Tattoo Guy. "The Eaters? That's what they are called? You've seen them too? You've seen what they do? You wouldn't! No, no. Don't leave me here."

"Then tell me who she is!" Jae points at me.

He panics and struggles against the rope, but gets nowhere. He gives up struggling and looks at me. "I really don't know who you are. I just recognised you from before. You and your group." **149**

"My group?"

"Your other group. With the children. You were the ones who kept taking our food."

"How many? How many in that group?"

"How should I know? I only remember you because of your hair. You and that red-headed girl. That's all I know! I don't know your name. I don't know who or what you are. I don't care! All I know is you have been trouble! Now let me go!" He is shouting.

"He knows nothing," Jae says, sighing. "We'd better go. We need to sleep."

I am so disappointed. I nod and we head for the front door.

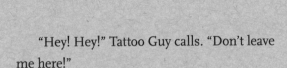

"Hey! Hey!" Tattoo Guy calls. "Don't leave me here!"

Jae and I look at each other.

"You will probably figure out the knots in a few hours. In the meantime, I suggest you keep as quiet as you can. The Eaters are attracted to sound," Jae tells him.

We go out and Jae locks the door from the outside.

"He should be safe enough in there. If he doesn't make any noise," Jae says.

I hesitate. Leaving a man helpless and tied up feels wrong. Even if he has tried to hurt me before. He is a real live man. A human being. Not one of those sick-looking Eaters.

"Don't worry," Jae assures me. "Those knots aren't tight. Anyway, his friends will surely come for him if he can't figure it out."

I hope he is right. He takes my hand and we walk silently back to the other house. We let ourselves in silently. I crash onto the sofa. I am spent. Emotionally and physically. I don't even complain when Jae squeezes himself next to me.

All 15 of us
are running.

We run through
the deserted streets,
glancing behind us
now and again. But
exhaustion starts to
take its toll and we
slow down.

"We have to stop
somewhere." I wheeze.
"I don't think we
can keep this up
much longer."

CHAPTER 32

Jae sighs, as much as someone can sigh when he's running. "I'm as tired as you are."

We have been alternating between running, jogging and walking for the past hour. We had started out as soon as it was light. We wanted to get away from those Eaters and Tattoo Guy as fast as we could.

"Does anyone know where we are?" It's Eryn.

I slow to a walk. I look around. We had taken the side streets, not wanting to expose ourselves on the wide open roads. Kyl had insisted that we make our way back east, towards Changi. Maybe, just maybe, he argued, they would let us back into Camp Zero.

After a few more minutes, we stop in front of a construction site for a luxury condo that looks newly completed.

There is a big sign with the words "FOR SALE", and an advertisement showing what the condo would have looked like had it been properly finished. One picture shows a beautiful apartment furnished with lush carpeting and wooden wall panelling. Others show a playground, a swimming pool, an orchid garden and a gym. The advertisement says the condo is a first-of-its-kind self-sustaining eco-condo. Whatever that means.

"Can we stay here?" Brion asks. "It looks deserted, and we haven't seen an Eater for ages."

The advertisement says there is a showflat. Jae volunteers to go look for it. He gestures to Dyanne to go with him. I look at him with some surprise. For some reason, I feel like shoving Dyanne's face into horse poop. Ten minutes pass and I begin to get irritated.

"Are you okay?" Eryn slips her hand into mine. "Don't be jealous. It's nothing."

Me? Jealous? Of Dyanne? Oh, please. Why would I be jealous of her? Uh, because she's with Jae, my ever-so-helpful inner voice says. And you like him. "I'm not jealous," I say.

Eryn smiles knowingly. I blush.

"Stop it, Eryn. I do not have a crush on Jae."

Jae chooses this moment to appear. "Huh? I heard my name. Is everything all right? Dyanne found the showflat, I never knew she was so good at..."

I walk away, not wanting to hear Jae praise Dyanne.

"You're such a boy," Eryn says to Jae, smacking his forehead.

"Ow!" Jae cries. "What did I do?"

Eryn whispers into his ear. She'd better not be telling him anything funny.

"Are you sure?" he says, glancing over at me.

I pretend to fiddle with my bag straps. That Eryn! What has she done?

"Anyway..." he says, turning back to address the group. "We found the showflat, let's go!"

He runs past me and ruffles my hair. "C'mon, rosebud!"

Rosebud? No way! But I can't help letting a smile find its way onto my face. I follow behind him, making sure the kids in my group are all there.

We run up the stairs, enthusiastically at first, but slowing down when we reach the fifth floor.

"Oh. My. God. How many more floors?" Brion asks.

"Just three more, you wimp," Jae calls from one flight above us.

"If I'm a wimp, you're a wuss," Brion says.

"If I'm a wuss, you're a fart head."

I giggle.

"When you fart, people in Africa die."

"When you fart, people have to call the firefighters."

"When you..."

"Too tired to play," Jae cuts in.

We reach the eighth level. There are only two apartments on each level. We step into the flat.

"Wow," I muse aloud. "Not bad. Not bad at all!"

There is a layer of dust everywhere, but we touch everything anyway. The living room is as the advertisement promised. Wood-panelled walls and carpeted floor. There is a huge L-shaped sofa that looks soft and plush. There is also an MV panel that takes up an entire wall, and it is hooked up to some fancy sound system, which I assume doesn't work.

CHAPTER 33

To the right is an open-plan kitchen, with just a counter separating it from the rest of the house. The kitchen looks fully equipped with fancy gadgets.

A corridor leads to the bedrooms. Some of the kids are already running into the rooms, squealing with excitement. I peek into one of them. It is fully furnished, with curtains, carpets and more wood panelling.

Nicky and two younger kids are jumping on the enormous king-sized bed. Something about their innocence makes me happy and sad at the same time. They are churning up dust that billows around the room. I sneeze and retreat outside.

Eryn runs up to me and tugs at my arm like a little child. "This is sooooo cool!" she says.

I smile at her joy. Life's little pleasures, right?

Brion goes to the glass doors on the other side of the living room. He slides them open and steps out into the balcony.

"There's a nice pool, just no water," he calls out.

Not that we are expecting any. I walk into the kitchen and notice a sink. I reach forward and turn on the tap anyway. Water gushes out of it. I yelp, surprised, and turn it off. I am ecstatic with my discovery and yell into the living room where Kyl has gathered everyone.

"THE SINK WORKS!" I shriek happily.

"The what?"

"Is she for real?"

"Water! From the tap!" I explain.

"OMG. How?" Brion jumps up and runs to the kitchen, screaming like a girl.

I giggle as he tries the tap. Again, water gushes out, clean and clear. Brion is gaping. The rest of the group lean over the counter, gaping as well.

"Turn it off!" Jae shouts. "You're wasting water!"

"What about the toilets?" Dyanne and Shulin ask. They run to check.

I hear flushing sounds. The toilets are working. I don't know where the water is coming from, and I am worried that it may run out.

"Hey guys," I say, peeking into the toilet in the first room, "maybe we should save the water for when we really need it?"

Kyl comes out from another room, holding a glossy brochure.

"The water is coming from a rain tank on the roof. They installed a filtration system to capture rainwater, filter it, and deliver it to the apartments," he says, reading from the brochure.

"And guess what?" he adds. "If this brochure is true, we may have electricity too, thanks to solar panels."

Everyone just about freaks out and runs to the nearest switch they can find.

I walk into the last room right at the end of the corridor. I gasp. It is a room most girls can only dream of. Canopy bed, frilly curtains, a giant MV panel, a high-end music player that is connected to tiny speakers around the room. And a weird roundish object.

I pick it up and stare at it. I find a button and press it tentatively. Suddenly, there's a little girl standing in front of me. Her pink flowery dress is torn and dirty. Her hair is all tangled. Tears stream down her face as she clutches a bunny soft toy.

"Help me," she pleads. "Mommy and Daddy haven't come back. They said they would find me food. I'm so hungry! I haven't eaten in three days."

She starts to sob, burying her face in her bunny. I reach out to smooth her hair back, but instead, my hand goes right through her head. I yelp and drop the object. She shimmers and disappears. I stand there in shock. I pick the object up and press the button again. The girl appears again and says the exact same thing. She's nothing but a projection. An illusion. A hologram.

I head for the door, tripping over my feet in excitement and shock.

I bump into Jae, who is on the way in. He looks disappointed.

"Anything work in here? Nothing works outside. Maybe the solar panels aren't connected yet. Or maybe they never got installed properly..." He stops jabbering when he sees my face.

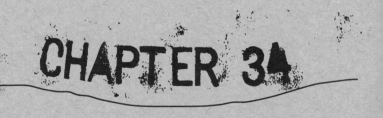

CHAPTER 34

I grab his hand and pull him into the room.

I hand him the object. "Press that button."

He does. The little girl reappears. His eyes widen, then he frowns as he watches the little girl cry.

"It's a hologram," Jae informs me.

"That girl. I think she was here?" I ask.

He hits the button again and this time, we look closely for clues to where the recording was done.

"It wasn't taken here," he says. "Look at the wall behind her. It is old and dirty."

"How did this end up here?" I ask.

"That's something we have to figure out. I don't like the idea that other people know about this place," Jae says thoughtfully.

"How does this thing work? I've never seen anything like it," I say as I take the device from him.

"This is old technology. My parents used to tell me about concerts they watched, where the singers were holograms. It was a Japanese thing, but the trend spread worldwide. Didn't your parents tell you about it?" Jae said.

I stared at him, annoyed.

"Oh, sorry. You don't remember." He looks sheepish.

"So this thing is old?"

"Yes, these holophones never took off. People could already video-chat. No one cared about sending

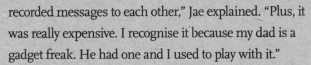

recorded messages to each other," Jae explained. "Plus, it was really expensive. I recognise it because my dad is a gadget freak. He had one and I used to play with it."

Jae suddenly looks very sad. This is the first time he's talked about his father. He fiddles with a dial and another projection pops up. This time the little girl doesn't have her bunny. She is cowering, her eyes huge with fear. I can almost hear her teeth chattering.

"They're coming for me," she whispers fearfully. "Mommy and Daddy are different now."

There's a pounding sound and she shudders. Then, a loud crushing noise.

"Oh, no." She gasps. "They got in."

A long bony hand grabs the little girl's arm and she screams. Her hologram fades.

Jae fiddles with the dial again and we see a new projection. It is the Eaters. They look ragged and desperate. I let out a small scream and cover my mouth. Jae puts one arm around my shoulders and pulls me close to him.

To my horror, I realise that one of them is holding a piece of a dress. A pink, flowery dress. But now it is stained with blood...

I know that Jae sees it too because he stiffens. The recording ends abruptly. It lasted only a few seconds, but it is enough for me to form some unwelcome conclusions. The Eaters eat humans. They hunt us and they eat us. If I wasn't sure before, I am certain now.

Jae turns to me. "We have to tell Kyl and the others. This is urgent."

"The kids too?"

"They have the right to see this," he says.

"But..."

Jae cuts me off. "They need to know. Gather them. Now."

I gather everyone into the bedroom. They are still excited and happy. I feel wretched about spoiling the mood.

"Sit on the bed," I order.

They sense my black mood and obey.

"What's going on?" Dyanne asks.

Jae starts the device. He plays all three projections. Even through I've already seen them, I can't help but shudder when I see the Eaters again. The younger kids scream when the Eaters pop into view. Eryn runs to grab me.

"What does this mean?" she says.

Kyl stands up when the recording ends. "This is bad. It looks like the Eaters are hunting children."

I see horror, fear, worry and disbelief – maybe even pity – etched on every face in the room.

"Wait. How do we know this is true?" It is Dyanne.

"She's right. This doesn't prove anything," the faithful sidekick Shulin speaks up too.

I glare at Dyanne. "How can this not be true?"

CHAPTER 35

"What if someone, you know, faked it? Maybe the Eaters were just pretending?" Dyanne says.

"If that's the case, tell me why that little girl looked so scared. Why would she fake that? Her fear was genuine," I say.

The room is tense, and our arguing is making it worse.

"Okay, okay," Brion says, trying to calm things down. "So if they are really hunting children, what does that mean for us? We continue running and hiding, right? Nothing changes."

"No," Kyl says. "Everything changes. If they are hunting us, we have to fight back."

Brion hesitates. "So we kill them?"

"No!" Eryn says immediately.

"I say, yes," Dyanne says.

A few of the children nod. Nicky has told them all about the Eaters in detail. They have seen the scar on his arm. They are scared and I don't blame them for wanting to kill the creatures.

"What if they can be saved? What if they can be turned back? Wouldn't it be killing innocent people?" Eryn continues.

She has a point. I look at Jae, who is looking right at me.

"Zee is the only one who has really seen them up close," he says. "She's the only one who has actually fought them. What do you think?"

What? Why me? I glare at Jae, mad at him for putting me on the spot like this. What does he expect me to say?

"I don't know."

"That's helpful," Dyanne says sarcastically.

"I don't know how to fight them. All I know is, they are attracted to sound. If we keep quiet, wouldn't we be safe?"

"Yes, you do!" It is little Nicky. Everyone is ganging up on me today. "I saw you fight them in the garden. I saw you! You were amazing. You killed them all!"

"I'm sure I didn't kill anyone," I say, alarmed. "I am not a murderer!"

I knocked some of the Eaters over, for sure. But I didn't think I had killed anyone. They got eaten by the others, but that didn't mean I had killed them.

"How about we trap one of them, and see what happens to him?" Brion suggests.

"That's a good idea," Kyl says. "And see what happens if we feed him. Or her."

"Oh? And how do you suppose we do that?" I scoff. No one here has any idea how disgusting those things are.

And how terrifying it is to be up close to them. "Who's going to catch him? The only place you'll end up is in the stomach of an Eater."

"We have to try, right?" Jae looks at me gently. "That's the only way for us to find out what exactly they are. And whether they can be saved."

"I agree," Kyl says.

"Me too," Brion says.

"I guess so," Eryn says reluctantly.

"Then, let's do it. Let's catch one and see what happens. If he tries to eat us, I'm killing him. Or her. Or it. And that's final," Dyanne says.

She speaks so forcefully that this time, no one disagrees.

"When do we do this?" I ask.

"Tomorrow. We do this tomorrow. Today, we rest. We shower. We recuperate," Kyl decides.

"Do we all have to go catch them?" Nicky wants to know.

"No, the younger ones will stay here. I don't want to put you guys in danger," Kyl says.

In theory, it is a good idea. And I do want to know what they are, and if they are still human. But someone has to be the one to catch an Eater. And somehow, I have the feeling that that someone is me.

The water on my face feels amazing. It is cold, but who cares. We are all taking turns to shower. I am the last in my group and I'm faintly worried that the water will run out. So I'm enjoying every second of the water as it pours out from the rain shower.

CHAPTER 36

Of course, no one had thought to bring
soap or shampoo, and the bottles displayed
on the shelf have turned out to be empty. So
I desperately try to comb out the tangles from
my waist-long hair. It is so grimy and there are
knots that just won't untangle. Oh well. At least
it is clean. It feels good to be clean.

I step out of the shower and pick up the
towel lying on the floor. There has only been
one towel hanging decoratively in each toilet.
Being the last one to shower definitely has its
disadvantages. I stare at the wet, grimy towel.
Dry myself with a dirty towel that's been used
by four other kids? Or stay wet? I choose
to stay wet. I rinse my underwear in the sink
and put them back on. I put on my spare set
of clothes.

The face that stares back in the mirror
looks haunted. There are huge bags under
my eyes. I wish – for the hundredth time – that
I could remember what happened to me.
I'm sure there is something I am supposed
to do.

I sigh and open the door and find Jae in
the room. He is on the bed telling three kids a
funny story. They are laughing.

I flop face down next to him. The bed feels heavenly. I feel him shift and his hands are on my back gently massaging me.

"What do we do, Jae?" I say.

"We'll figure something out, pussy willow."

What? What did he call me?

I turn around and look at him, affronted. "Hey! That was rude."

"No, it's not! Pussy willow is the name of a very special plant," he says.

"Well, it sounds rude," I say. I bite my lip to stifle a giggle but I fail and let out a very loud, very piggy-sounding snort instead. The kids burst into laughter. I can't help but laugh too, rolling up into a ball and clutching my stomach.

"How would you like it if I called you a pussy willow?" I say. "Next time you call me that, I'll push you into a pool."

Jae's eyes widen. He shakes me by my shoulders. "Zee! You're a genius!"

I look around. "Huh? What did I do? Er, I mean... Darn right, I'm a genius."

He shoots me a grin that makes my heart beat faster.

"We lure them into the pool."

So the plan is set.
We all gather around
the pool downstairs.
It is a small kidney-
shaped pool, more
for relaxing than
for doing actual
laps. It would have
been beautiful, I
muse, had it been
completed. Only the
bottom had been
tiled. The workers
never got round to
putting tiles onto the
sides of the pool.

CHAPTER 37.

The boys have found some construction planks and made a wobbly bridge across the pool. The plan: Someone is to stand in the middle of the pool and make loads of noise. The Eaters will come, walk towards the noise, and fall into the pool. Again, good idea in theory. In reality, not such a good idea, because that someone is going to be me.

I have to be the bait. And if something goes wrong, I'll end up being eaten. Not a very nice mental image. Or, I could walk onto the plank, and it breaks, and I die. Then my remains get eaten.

Jae comes up to me and gives me a hug. "Are you sure you want to do this?"

"Yes," I insist. I don't know why, but I know that this is something I have to do.

Kyl and Brion have gone to the main road to see if they can spot any of the Eaters. They are supposed to target a lone Eater and lure him here quietly. They have been gone for more than two hours. I am beginning to get worried.

Eryn is pacing. She runs over to me. "Do you think they are okay?"

"I'm sure they are," I say, even though I don't know for sure. I give her a hug.

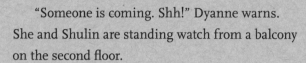

"Someone is coming. Shh!" Dyanne warns. She and Shulin are standing watch from a balcony on the second floor.

"I see Brion running. Kyl is right behind him. Oh no," says Shulin.

Oh no? Why oh no?

"There are so many of them!" Dyanne shouts from above.

"How many?" Jae asks.

"More than 10," she says.

To Eryn, she orders, "Get back to the apartment and make sure the little ones stay there. Lock the door, and no matter what, do not open it! Understand?"

"But Brion..." Eryn begins.

"Brion will be fine. I promise," I tell Eryn. "Go!"

She runs off just when Brion and Kyl come tearing into the pool area.

"Okay, everyone, stand by!" Kyl shouts. "Zee, there's a group approaching. Go for it! And good luck! Be careful out there!"

I nod. Maybe this is a bad idea. I walk out onto the middle of the bridge and crouch down to keep my balance. Well, it's way too late to back out now.

The first Eater shuffles in just as Kyl, Brion and Jae arm themselves with planks. They stand close by, not making a sound. These Eaters are moving much faster and seem more alert than the last group we encountered back at the house.

"Over here, you smelly worthless thing. OVER HERE!" I shout.

They turn to me and start moving towards me faster than I expected. They're so close I can smell them. Their shuffling gets faster and they approach me from the front. My heart thuds in my chest.

"You cannot get me! You cannot get me!" I taunt them.

Their grunts and animal growls are giving me the creeps. There are both men and women, but the only way I can tell them apart is from their clothes. There is nothing recognisably human about them. The skin on their faces is raw and bloody. And they have no hair. I try to see if there is any spark of life or humanity in their eyes, but honestly, I see none.

"Hey, you! Over here!" I continue to shout.

They follow the sound of my voice and inch towards the pool. Come on, come on. Just a few more steps.

"Hey, you! Your mama so fat, when she sits around the house, she sits *around* the house!"

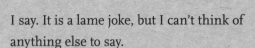

I say. It is a lame joke, but I can't think of anything else to say.

Behind me, Jae snorts with laughter. The Eaters at the front shift their attention towards him. I turn and glare at him and gesture at him to be quiet.

"Hey! Over here, you uglies! Your mama so fat, when she fell in love, she broke it!" I shout, desperate to turn their attention away from Jae and the others.

"Your mama so fat, when she laughs, the people in Indonesia feel an earthquake."

Much to my relief, they turn towards me and the first ones tumble into the pool. One by one, they follow, falling in a heap at the bottom of the pool. I heave a sigh of relief.

I take a step back. I feel for the plank without looking. Ah, there it is.

But I trip and fall.

"Zee!" I hear Jae shout softly. "Be careful."

I manage to grab the plank with one hand and struggle to pull myself up. The Eaters that have fallen are getting closer and closer.

This can't be the end, can it?

I push that thought out of my mind and muster all the strength I can gather. I feel a hand brush my leg and I have to bite my lip to stop myself from screaming. I give one last pull and yank my body back onto the plank. I stare at the woman Eater below. She hisses at me. She has no teeth.

Not daring to stand up, I crawl on all fours along the plank till I reach the other side of the pool where Jae is waiting. He rubs my back reassuringly.

The Eaters are all reaching out of the pool, desperately trying to clamber out. I make eye contact with one of them and gasp. His eyes are blank, but they are green. And familiar. I backpedal slowly.

"Which one are we going to take?" Kyl asks.

"That one," I say straightaway, pointing to the Eater with the green eyes.

"Okay," Kyl says. "Jae and I will do this. The rest of you, go back upstairs and keep watch. Just in case there are more Eaters."

CHAPTER 38

No, no, no! Not Jae. What if he gets hurt? What if he gets eaten? What if he dies? I am gripped with a sudden panic. What if I lose Jae?

"No," I say. "I'm going to help."

"Don't worry," Jae says. "We've got it figured out. We don't even have to touch them."

He and Kyl have fashioned a hooking device out of wood and ropes. They plan to hook an Eater by the neck. Hook an Eater by the neck? I am reminded of an old nursery song... *Eeny meeny minee mo, catch a spider by the toe.* Hook an Eater by the neck. *If he cries, let him go... Eeny meeny minee mo.*

No. Stop it, Zee. Stop it! I feel I am going crazy.

A voice snaps me back to reality. "Zee? Zee, are you listening to me?"

I shake my head and look at Jae. He is looking at me with a rather amused look on his face.

"Huuuh?" I say.

"I said is that okay with you?"

"Oh." I hesitate. If Jae can't do this, no one else can. So reluctantly, I nod my head slowly in agreement.

"B-But be careful, okay!" I stammer. "Don't die! Promise me you won't die!"

Jae chuckles softly. "I promise I won't die."

I reach out and touch his face. He places his hand over mine and stares into my eyes.

"Be safe, all right?" I whisper, pulling my hand out of his grip.

He nods, looking serious and a little scared. "Don't worry. I can take care of myself."

I throw my arms around him and I feel him stiffen before relaxing and hugging me back.

"I'll be fine," he tells me.

I run up the stairs, back to the apartment on the eighth floor. When Eryn sees me and Brion, she yelps with joy, hugging each of us in turn. She hugs Dyanne and Shulin too. I rush to the balcony to look down into the pool area.

My breath catches in my throat as I watch Jae and Kyl approach the pool. Jae draws the lasso back and hooks one of them – the green-eyed one – around his neck. He gives the rope one quick yank and the Eater comes out.

He lunges at Jae and Jae stumbles back, a little surprised. My eyes go wide and I swear my heart stops beating.

Kyl swings from behind, hitting the back of the Eater's knees. The Eater keels over. Not wasting a second, Kyl jumps up immediately and secures his hands behind him. Jae then takes

his rope and binds the Eater's legs together. I see
him hesitate for a second, probably wondering
whether he should release the noose around the
Eater's neck. He doesn't.

Mission completed. He looks up at us and
gives us two thumbs up.

Behind him, in the pool, the grunts of
the other Eaters get louder. I retreat into the
apartment, where the sound is muted.

I heave a sigh of relief when they come back. Jae grins at me, pleased with himself.

"I got him! Be careful though, he's a lunger."

I frown. A lunger?

"Come and see. We've put him in the gym next to the pool."

CHAPTER 39

Dyanne and Shulin insist on staying with the kids, so only Brion, Eryn and I go down.

As soon as I enter the gym, the Eater snarls at me and lunges forward, trying to grab me. I jump a mile in the air and back away. He can't reach me though. He is secured to one of the gym machines by the noose around his neck.

Jae laughs. "I told you he is a lunger."

I give Jae a weird look and think he has the strangest sense of humour. I stare at the Eater. His eye sockets are torn and bloody and he's missing an ear. There are pockets of pus and blisters on his face and there is a long gash down the side of his face.

His face is the colour of rotting tofu and there are maggots crawling out of his nose. It makes me want to gag. His hair is lank and probably tick-infested. Long greasy strands hang around his face. His arms are covered in bruises and cuts. But that isn't the worst part. The worst part is his smell. I have to breathe through my mouth and I can taste it. God, I want to throw up.

Brion comes in, followed by Eryn. The moment she does, the Eater starts going crazy. Growling and hissing and trying to get free, he lunges in Eryn's direction. She screams, trying to get as far away as possible. I hear a crack and suddenly his hands are free. His thumbs hang loosely from his hands. He has broken his thumbs to escape the rope binding his wrists.

He lunges forward again and tries to grab Eryn. But he is held back by the noose.

Brion is hugging Eryn, who is screaming.

I walk over to her and take her hand. "Shh, it's okay. It can't get you."

She nods, swallows and takes a deep breath.

An idea forms in my head. I take Eryn by the hand and walk silently to the other side of the gym. The Eater's head swivels as we walk. I leave Eryn in the corner and walk away from her. The Eater ignores me and continues lunging in Eryn's direction.

"He can smell her," I say. "That's how they hunt younger children."

Eryn yelps and runs out of the gym. Brion follows close behind. I look at Kyl and Jae. This new development is highly worrying. If they can smell children, we are not safe.

I hand Kyl a small tin of sardines I had taken from our stash. He pulls the tab and opens it. He puts it on the floor and kicks it in the Eater's direction.

We watch as the Eater follows the sound of the tin. He reaches for it, but can't find it. Jae inches over quietly, picks up the tin, and places it in the Eater's hand. His hand brushes the Eater's and he shudders.

The Eater sniffs at the tin, then flings it across the room. We all glance at each other in confusion. He sniffs the place on his hand where Jae has touched him. A rotten-looking tongue pokes out of his mouth. He licks his own hand.

I look at Jae and gasp. "He's going to..."

"Eat himself," Jae continues.

The Eater sniffs his hand again and sinks his teeth into his own hand.

I let out a gasp and look at Jae. I start shaking. "Stop him!" I yell at Jae. "Why is he doing that?!"

The Eater takes another bite of his arm. His blood drips down his arm and he slurps it up greedily. I feel sick. I can't watch this anymore. I stumble out of the room and slump down against the wall.

I put my head in between my knees. Calm down, Zee. Calm down. Slowly, slowly, I count my heartbeats. I get to 140 beats per minute before I manage to stand up. Jae and Kyl have shut the gym door behind them. They wedge it tight with

a plank. Both look exhausted. We go back upstairs silently. Every step seems harder to take than the last.

We walk into the living room where the kids are looking at us hopefully. Brion and Eryn look grim. They haven't told the others anything.

"So, did he eat? What did he say?" Dyanne asks.

Kyl shakes his head.

"Well, what happened?" Dyanne demands.

Kyl takes a big breath. "He didn't eat. It doesn't look like they can be saved. I... I think they have to be killed."

I notice that he doesn't tell them what happened with Eryn. He doesn't want to scare them. I look at Eryn and Brion and shake my head. They understand. We mustn't tell the kids. Why scare them more than they already are?

"Are you sure?" a little girl asks sadly.

"Yes," I reply. "We are sure."

"Can't we let him go?" she continues.

"I don't think so, Emma." Jae says. He looks a bit uncomfortable. "I'm sorry. He started... eating himself."

Horrified gasps fill the room.

"They're attracted to smell. He ate the part where I touched him," Jae continues. "He totally ignored the real food."

"So they crave only human flesh?" Dyanne deduces. "Great, just great!"

"What about those in the pool?" Emma asks.

"We have to destroy them," Kyl says. "Tomorrow."

Brion closes the sliding door leading to the balcony and draws the curtains. That way, no one can see or hear the Eaters. We all know that come morning, we will have to kill them and none of us can feel good about that. We file silently into the bedrooms and huddle up on the giant beds, grateful we are not alone.

In the morning, Brion and Eryn stay behind with the kids while Kyl, Jae, Dyanne, Shulin and I go downstairs to destroy the Eaters. We have told Dyanne and Shulin about how they can smell younger children, and we all agree that the kids should be kept as far away from the Eaters as possible.

CHAPTER 40

We figure fire will be the best way to do it. Jae has two boxes of matches while Kyl has found lots of old boxes that will serve well as kindling. We edge towards the pool cautiously. It is so quiet.

"Are they sleeping?" I whisper to Jae.

"I hope so," Jae says.

He places his hand on my back. It is the only thing anchoring me to reality. When we reach the pit, we freeze in shock. The Eaters are gone.

Well, not totally gone. There are only two Eaters left. And they are eating each other. All that's left in the pit are bones.

I try desperately to suck in the breaths I need.

"Zee? Calm down. Shh. It'll be okay." Jae rubs my back and leads me away.

I look up at the balcony and see the horrified look on the kids' faces. They shouldn't be seeing this! Kyl waves at them to go inside, but they don't move. They are looking at something else in the distance. They look even more horrified than before.

"Oh no, not more of them," I say to Jae.

We run to the balcony on the second level to have a better view.

It is a small group of teenagers and children. They are all on skateboards, fleeing from a horde of Eaters. I see a boy with white hair jump over a trash bin and whip his skateboard from under his feet, hitting an Eater in the face before landing and skating away.

I see an Asian-looking boy do a tricky manoeuvre over a curb. He whips his legs around and kicks three Eaters down. Another boy jumps into the air and kicks an Eater away, clutching his board with his right hand before landing and zooming off. A red-haired girl leaps into the air and lands on one of the Eaters. Even the younger kids jump onto cars with their boards and skate out of danger.

There is something familiar about the way the white-haired boy moves, though I don't know why. Once, he looks like he is going to crash right into a car. Instead, he leaps from his skateboard, flies over the roof of the car, and lands back on his skateboard which has travelled to the other side. It is very, very cool.

We all watch in amazement as they get closer and closer to our condo. The kids stop right outside the compound of the condo and look up. We duck down behind the balcony wall and hope that those on the eighth floor do the same.

"Why are we hiding?" I point out.

Dyanne glares at me. "More people means more mouths. Do you see them carrying food?"

"But they look normal! We have to meet them! Strength in numbers! Don't you think we would survive better as a bigger group?" I point out.

"Look at how much trouble just one of you has brought us. We were happy until you came," Dyanne says. "You have brought us nothing but bad luck."

"Hey!" Jae steps in. "She's also helped us. You can't blame what happened with the Eaters on her! Without her, we could all be dead!"

There is a scream and we all stand up to look. One of the children in that group has been taken by an Eater. It is a girl and she looks so small in the arms of a huge Eater.

"Let me go," she screams.

The others all turn around to help. But they don't see what we see. Coming from a side street, hidden from their view, is a group of about 20 Eaters. In addition to the Eaters coming down towards them from the other direction, I estimate there must be 50 of them. Against eight kids. It doesn't seem fair.

I gape at Jae. "We have to help them! Please!"

Jae nods. "I'll come with you."

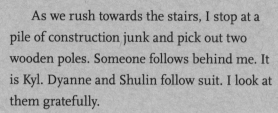

As we rush towards the stairs, I stop at a pile of construction junk and pick out two wooden poles. Someone follows behind me. It is Kyl. Dyanne and Shulin follow suit. I look at them gratefully.

"You don't have to do this if you don't want to," I say.

I just get stony faces from Dyanne and Shulin. Kyl shrugs.

Jae lays his hand on my shoulder. "Let's go."

We sprint down the stairs, taking three at a time. When we reach them, we can see only five kids. The two guys – the white-haired one and the Asian-looking one – are fending off the Eaters while the girl with the flaming red hair is protecting two kids who look no older than eight.

CHAPTER 41.

I thought kids that young didn't survive. I'm pretty shocked. I don't know whether to be happy or sad. Jae and Kyl jump in to help right away. The newcomers look at us with some surprise, but there is no time for words. There are too many Eaters.

Jae effortlessly knocks down two Eaters with his pole. Left, right. I didn't realise what a good fighter he is. He jumps into the air and whips his stick around so that all four Eaters advancing towards us fall.

"Go look for the others. Kyl and I can take care of these ones here. There are only a few left."

A few? My eyes widen.

"Are you crazy?" I yell as I jab my stick into an Eater's head. "I'm not leaving you here."

"There were three more kids! You have to find them!"

Then what he does surprises me. He grabs my shoulders and kisses me. Sparks fly as his lips press against mine. I swear my heart literally stops beating. I realise what's happening and kiss him back. Time slows around us and it's just the two of us. No one trying to eat us, no problems, no confusion. We break apart and I stare into his amazingly beautiful green eyes.

"Go, please," he whispers.

He is right. I reluctantly let him go and peer around to see where the other three have gone. I smack three Eaters out of the way easily and run to where I can see down the side street. I see a different crowd of Eaters dragging three kids away – two of them look my age. The third child is the girl who had first gotten caught. She is screaming. I count almost 20 Eaters.

"Dyanne! Shulin! Over here!"

As I sprint towards the Eaters, I scream to get their attention. The Eaters turn towards me. I feel that familiar tingle. This time, it starts in my fingertips and travels all the way up my arms, spreading down my belly and up my spine. I relax into the sensation and let instincts take over.

My hands spin the pole. Faster and faster it goes. It confuses the Eaters. A quick flick brings down an Eater to the right and another to the left. I spin the pole over my head and bring it sweeping down over three more. Their heads crunch under the weight of the pole. They growl in agony. Five down, how many more to go?

I see Dyanne and Shulin fending off one each. They are both clumsy and unused to fighting. Thankfully, the Eaters are slow-moving and dull.

Dyanne punches one right in the nose, which sort of disintegrates.

"Ew! Ew!" she yells as she pulls her hand back. It is covered with slime.

Shulin is struggling with her Eater. She kicks at it, but it is such a feeble kick. The Eater grabs her neck and pulls her head to his mouth. She screams.

Dyanne looks over in horror. She runs over but is blocked by two Eaters.

"Shulin! Shulin!" The dread in her voice goes right to my heart. The Eater opens its mouth to bite.

I race over, knowing I won't be able to reach her in time. Grasping my pole like a javelin, I aim and release. The pole flies in an arc, landing right in the Eater's eye. Its head snaps back and it falls over. Shulin falls over too, landing on it. I run over to help her up.

"Are you okay?" My voice is high-pitched and loud.

She nods.

"Stay with me," I order her. I can't leave her alone if she can't fight. She'll be dead meat, literally.

I grab Shulin's hand and head back to the group of Eaters shambling slowly away with the three kids. I scream again to get their attention.

"Hey, you stupids! Come and get me!" I shout.

CHAPTER 42

They don't seem to care. They are fixated on the smell of the young girl. I need to find something they want more. Something that will make them let go of the child. I slide a small knife out from my pocket. I close my eyes, grit my teeth and slash down hard along the side of my arm. The pain is instant. I scream.

Holding up my bleeding arm, I shout, "How about this! Want some of this blood?"

Behind me, Shulin says, "Are you crazy?"

Am I? Probably.

In any case, it works. The smell of my blood energises the Eaters. They drop the girl and the two others, and lurch towards me. Their movements are jerky and awkward, but they are motivated. By my blood. I turn around and push Shulin away from me. She is safe, now that all they want is me.

I smile as I twirl my pole. I am so ready for them. Again, my body takes over and I watch my arms and legs move of their own accord. I sweep the pole, knocking two Eaters off their feet. Two more reach out for me, but they each get a blow to their throats and they fall down.

Left, right, twirl, smash. Double twirl, tap, tap. They fall down one by one. But they keep coming. I am getting tired. I pause for a breath and see Jae, Kyl and the five new kids running my way. Thank goodness. I can do with some help. I am surrounded by the Eaters, and the only thing holding them back is my pole.

The white-haired boy is screaming a strange battle cry, "Kay! Kay! Kay!" The others in his group join in. What a bunch of weirdos.

Then the white-haired boy throws his skateboard on the ground and jumps on it, propelling himself towards me.

"Kay!" he yells. "Vee!"

Huh? Is this the time for some alphabet game? What does he mean?

There is panic on his face when I don't respond.

"Vee! Vee!" he yells at me. "V position!"

My arms move on their own. I swing the pole one more time, making a swinging circle that keeps the Eaters away. Then, even though I don't know why, I plant the pole vertically down on the ground and brace it against my right shoulder. My legs are bent, ready to take the impact.

Just in time.

The boy kicks the back of his skateboard and launches himself into the air, over the heads of the Eaters.

"Incoming!" he yells as he reaches for my pole.

I feel his weight as he grabs my pole to swing himself around. He is going so fast the momentum swings him around once, twice, three times. Each time he goes around, I hear sickening sounds – crunching and splattering. At last, he lands next to me. I straighten up and look around me. All the Eaters are down, either dead or dying.

I gape at him in shock. I hear a ringing in my ears and the world seems to be contracting. Something is squeezing my brain.

I blink and try to ask for help, but I can't get the words out. He looks at me in alarm and reaches out to catch me as I fall. What beautiful green eyes he has...

"Kayla, wake up!
Wake up! Please
hurry! Hurry!
They're coming!
You have to go."

Around me is smoke,
the building is on
fire. I choke on
smoke and my eyes
water. I blink rapidly,
trying to clear my
eyes. I spot Dev and
Lily dragging the kids
out while Connor is
shaking me.

CHAPTER 43

"They're after you, Kayla. RUN." He tries to
pull me out from under the cupboard.

*"Come on!" he shouts, before coughing. I yank
my arm out from underneath and scream as I scrape
my wrist.*

*"Come on! You can do it," he screams. I notice
he is crying. "Please."*

*Part of the ceiling collapses next to me and I look
up at Connor fearfully. More debris falls, this time on
my head.*

"Go on without me," I rasp.

Images rush through my head. I scream and
jolt awake. I am breathing heavily. Jae is standing
over me and is looking at me with concern.

"Are you okay?" he asks.

I look at my hand and see the fading scar of a
scrape on my wrist. I look at Jae. I look past him
to all the young survivors forming a circle around
me. The ones from our group, and the eight new
ones. We are all back in the apartment on the
eighth floor. Everyone has crowded into the living
room, worry in their eyes.

I straighten up, struggling to get air into my
lungs. I look up at Jae fearfully.

"What's going on?" I ask.

"It's okay. We are all okay," he says.

"Who are they?" I ask, pointing at the new kids.

The red-haired girl looks amazed. "Is that really you? What happened? How did you get out? We thought you were dead!"

I frown. I feel a tingle, stronger than ever. But I push it away.

Get out? Get out from where?

The white-haired boy says nothing. He just walks forward and hugs me. I hug him back awkwardly for, like, a second, before pushing him away. Jae sits down protectively next to me.

I look into the white-haired boy's eyes and I jerk away in shock. Those green eyes.

"I've missed you so much," he says. He is struggling not to cry.

I gasp and back away, knocking into Jae. He slides an arm around my waist. I am so confused.

"You don't remember me?" the boy with the white hair asks, his face hardening.

"I-I don't know. I don't remember anything," I stammer.

Jae tightens his grip on me.

"You were one of us. Don't you remember? I'm Connor, that's Dev and she's Lily."

Dev? Connor? Lily? I was one of them?

"I-I-I don't know what you're talking about."
I shake my head. "I really don't. I'm sorry."

"Nothing? At all? Do you remember the fire?"
It is the red-haired girl, Lily.

"The fire? You mean that was real?" I look at
the scar on my wrist again.

Jae snaps his head at me. "What fire?"

"That fire was real," Connor says, looking at
Jae's arm around my waist. "I-I-I... I tried to get
you out, but the fire was too big. We tried to get
help, but by the time we came back, the fire had
burnt out, and you were gone. We thought they
took you away. We looked for you for days..."

"It's true. We looked everywhere, but you
were gone," Dev joins in. "Kay, how could you
forget us? How could you forget Connor?"

I suddenly reach forward and touch Connor's
face on impulse. Then I yank my hand away,
eyes wide.

"It's late. She remembers nothing. You should
stop interrogating her. Let's get some rest." It is
Dyanne that comes to my rescue.

I smile gratefully at her.

"She's right," Jae says. "Let's get some rest."
He stands up and pulls me to him. I lean into him,
but my feelings are all jumbled and confused.

Lily marches up to me and puts both hands on my shoulders.

"Kay, please. We've missed you so much. Connor especially. Can't you tell? His beautiful black hair has turned white!" she says.

I stare at Connor in shock. His hair used to be black? Connor glances back at me wearily.

I feel a sharp pain at the back of my head. I smell smoke and start to gasp for breath. Connor looks at me. There are tears in his green eyes.

"Please, Kayla," Connor says.

I look up at Jae. I look into his green eyes. I look at Connor again.

There's that squeezing sensation in my head again and my world contracts. I close my eyes. A memory bubbles up and I literally hear a pop in my head.

My eyes fly open.

Finally, finally, I remember everything.

TO BE CONTINUED...

I remember now.

I remember how.

I remember why.

I remember what
I must do.

But who am I?

Zee - the person I thought I was? Or Kayla - the person I am supposed to be?

I am both yet neither. Then there's Jae. And then there is Connor.

One more thing - we are running out of food. And the Eaters are still after us.

Do we continue to run?
Or is it time to hide?

HIDE

Read the continuing story in the second
instalment of this series.

COMING SOON IN 2014

FIND OUT MORE

WWW.RUNHIDESEEK.COM

**Like runhideseek on Facebook
or follow runhideseek on Tumblr and Twitter**

- Get updates on the Run Hide
  Seek series

- Read interviews with the author

- Be the first to know about events
  and appearances

- Take part in the "Shoot a Trailer"
  contest to win cash prizes

RUN BY GABBY TYE IS AVAILABLE
AS AN EBOOK FROM
ALL GOOD EBOOK STORES.

ACKNOWLEDGEMENTS

I would like to thank Aunty Elaine for reading my first drafts and giving helpful suggestions. Also, a big thank you to Aunty Elise, who read and re-read each version of my story, spotting and correcting errors along the way.

A heartfelt note of appreciation also goes out to my teachers and friends who read my story and encouraged me, including: Mr Vincent Chia (my primary school English teacher), Miss Grace Khoo (my secondary school English teacher), Rachel Liam, See Shuen Ning, Chloe Sng, Ceres Foo, Elizabeth Ho, Shernis Ong, Chloe Koo, Dana Chua, Liao Peiru and Yukie Foong.

For the use of his amazing photo on the back cover of this book, I would like to thank Nicholas Chew. More of his photos can be seen on www.flickr.com/photos/donkey32123/ and www.facebook.com/nicchewphotography

ABOUT THE AUTHOR

Gabby Tye likes the feeling of speed and the wind through her hair. She gets her adrenalin rush from rollerblading, skateboarding, riding on roller coasters and leaping off high places (while tethered to a safety harness).

Gabby, 14, lives in Singapore where she spends most of her time on Tumblr. She also is unnaturally absent-minded and would like to know if anyone has seen her mobile phone.